The Billionaire's Surrogate

What started as a pregnancy of convenience could soon be a lot more...

A complete story with no cliff hanger.

Money is nothing without someone to love.

Max is a billionaire with a lot going for him. He has the money, the looks, and a personality to boot. But when diagnosed with prostate cancer, his life turns around in an instant.

Everything that was once important now seems trivial to him, and he soon realizes he hasn't achieved his one main goal in life:

Having a baby.

With his cancer treatment predicted to leave him sterile, he decides hiring a surrogate mother to bare his child is the best option. And

Christine, a relative of his house keeper, agrees to the role.

But soon after the process, further tests reveals Max doesn't have cancer after all and won't become infertile. Now the question of where this leaves him and Christine arises.

Will she simply remain the mother of his child? Or will an even more personal relationship form from this unexpected turn of events?

Find out in this touching love filled romance by Cher Etan.

Suitable for over 18s only due to passionate love making scenes likely to leave you needing a cold shower.

Don't miss out, get your copy now.

Get Free Romance eBooks!

Hi there. As a special thank you for buying this book, for a limited time I want to send you some great ebooks completely **free of charge** directly to your email! You can get it by going to this page:

www.SaucyRomanceBooks.com/RomanceBooks

www.saucyromancebooks.com/physical

You can see a the cover of these books on the next page:

These ebooks are so exclusive you can't even buy them. When you download them I'll also send you updates when new books like this are available.

Again, that link is:

www.saucyromancebooks.com/physical

ISBN-13: 978-1514380437

ISBN-10: 1514380439

Contents

Chapter 1

"Dear all, we are gathered here today to celebrate the nuptials between Christine Alexandre Richards and Rudy Sinclair. If anyone has any objection as to why these two individuals should not be joined in Holy Matrimony, please speak up now or forever hold your peace," the priest said solemnly. He was inexplicably dressed in a red jumpsuit and had on make up. In fact, he looked very much like RuPaul if Christine was not mistaken. Still it was her wedding day and she was ecstatic.

"I object," the voice said, again and again and again, that voice always objected. No matter what other details of the wedding changed, that one remained the same. Slowly even though she tried to stop herself doing it, Christine turned around. It felt like one of those slow motion scenes in movies when something horrible is going to happen and the heroine is only in time to turn around with a scream and shout "No" in that slow motion voice that sounded like a nineties tape recorder when the tape stuck. The woman was always standing there dressed head to toe in yellow...*yellow;* such a festive color to choose to go around breaking up people's weddings...and their hearts. She was a white woman, taller than average and curvy. In fact her ass was just about the curviest thing Christine had ever seen…and she'd grown up in an African American neighborhood so she should know. She wore high yellow heels, they were almost golden in fact and her toes were gaily painted blue. She had on a hat…with a veil. The veil just barely covered her blue eyes and her red lined smiling lips were staring cruelly and mercilessly at Christine as she voiced her objection. When she was sure she had everyone's attention in the room she sauntered over to the altar and slipped her hand through Rudy's. He seemed to be frozen to the spot and didn't object.

"You can't marry him because he's already mine," the woman said with a triumphant smile.

It was always at this point that Christine startled awake in a cold sweat; the dream that wasn't a dream *not* fading conveniently but echoing as if continuing in some other dimension close by.

"Rudy," she would whisper in despair and then get out of bed to go rinse her face and get herself a glass of water.

"Bad dream?" her grandmother would ask, coming out of her room when Christine did. Christine would shrug like it was nothing and go to the kitchen. Her grandmother would follow and begin heating some milk for hot chocolate.

"You don't have to do that," Christine would say.

"I know," her grandmother would reply, eyes on the milk to make sure it didn't boil over.

*****

Max Lestrange was in the front row, sitting next to his beautiful model date, he was pretty sure her name was Kendal but he wasn't a hundred percent positive of that. They were here to watch the big fight as guests of the mayor of Las Vegas. Max was good friends with her husband. He had been like a father figure to him as he learned the ropes of being an attorney at law and in turn Max had supported him when he and then his wife, had run for office. The press was out in force because the match was a big deal between the defending champion and his closest contender. Max was trying to enjoy himself but it had been a strange day; perhaps he was getting old because all he wanted to do was lie down. The wine he'd taken with dinner was making him dizzy and not in a good way and the room was hot in spite of the air conditioning. He could feel the sweat on his forehead and his upper lip. He really was not liking himself today and wished he could just excuse himself and go lie down. The match was starting though and servers were coming around with more champagne. Maybe that would make him feel better. He took a glass and downed it at once, more for the cold wetness than the taste but it did not make him feel better at all. In fact if he was honest it made him feel queasy and nauseous. He was afraid that he would have to excuse himself soon if things did not settle down on their own. Kendal or Kim or whatever her name was leaned toward him with a smile, murmuring something about how exciting it was. Max murmured something suitable in reply and then leaned over to speak with the mayor.

"Carolyn, I have to excuse myself," he said standing up fighting the wave of dizziness that assailed him. He really needed to lie down.

"Oh, what's up?" Carolyn asked.

Max opened his mouth to reply but then the world was replaced with darkness and he knew no more.

*****

He woke to a beeping sound and the feel of a cool breeze on his buttocks. He had difficulty opening his eyes, they seemed welded shut...that or he had no eyes any longer.

"Hallo," he croaked still trying valiantly to open his eyes. "Anybody there?"

"Mr. Lestrange sir, you're awake," the voice of his housekeeper said sounding relieved. "I'll get the nurse."

"Martha wait," he said sharply and felt her stop moving. "What's wrong with my eyes?"

"Oh, they applied some sort of paste over them, I think to stop them fluttering...you were convulsing sir. Anyway, I'll get the nurse," Martha said.

Max waited impatiently for someone to come and tell him what was going on with him. He continued to try and open his eyes. He thought of wiping the paste off with his hands but when he tried to move them, he felt a pinprick of pain and a pulling sensation he didn't like so he ceased to do that forthwith.

"Ah, Mr. Lestrange, welcome back to the land of the living," a low male voice said to him, sounding too familiar for someone he'd never met.

"And you are?" he asked coldly.

"I'm doctor Schofield, your physician," the voice said.

"I see," Max replied. "And what exactly is wrong with me?"

"We're not sure yet," the doctor replied breezily.

"Could you remove this paste so I can open my eyes?" Max asked irritably.

"Of course. Nurse?" the doctor's voice said. After a moment, Max felt a cool cloth wiping him gently around his eyes. He could feel whatever was holding his eyes closed loosen its hold and suddenly he could see again, his eyes were open and he was staring at Martha, his black housekeeper for nigh on fifteen years now, and a young man with black hair and vivid blue eyes who was wearing a white lab coat. He was also smiling at him as if he couldn't be more pleased with himself. Max hated him on sight.

"So you don't know what's wrong with me, why am I here?" he asked coldly.

Dr. Schofield's smile faltered a bit but it came back, almost at full wattage. "We're running tests. Your temperature was elevated very high when you came in. So much so that you were convulsing. You almost went into shock but we pulled you back. You're white blood cell count is also elevated which means you're sporting an infection of some kind. Hopefully once the blood work comes back we'll know more."

Max stared into the middle distance. "I see," he said. "My doctor's name is Carlyle Benson; I'm sure my housekeeper's told you. Would you kindly summon him?"

"Your housekeeper did inform us of your doctor's name and the fact that you would want him – but he is not affiliated with this hospital and so-"

"Then move me to a facility with which he *is* affiliated," Max interrupted.

That at least wiped the smile off Dr. Schofield's face. "Mr. Lestrange you have to know that you are very weak right now and not in any position to be moved," he said in a more subdued tone than he'd been hitherto using. "It would not behoove you to try and do so. At least wait until you're stronger."

Max glared at him, wanting to punch him in the face but truly feeling too weak to move. He hated it, this weakness; and it scared the hell out of him. What had happened to him?

"Have you checked my system for drugs?" he asked.

"It's one of the tests requested," Dr. Schofield said. "If you can be just a little patient we should know in an hour or two what ails you."

"An hour or two?" Max exclaimed in disbelief.

"We ordered extensive tests sir," Dr. Schofield said.

Max just glared at him, wanting to get out of bed, possibly hit something; preferably the good doctor. But he just lay back in defeat and stared at the ceiling.

"Martha, did you bring my bed clothes?" he asked.

"Yes sir, right here," Martha said placing a pair of pajamas on the bedside table where Max could see them.

"Can I at least change out of this mortifying gown?" Max asked the doctor.

Dr. Schofield opened his mouth to explain hospital policy but then closed it again. This level of politics was above his pay grade. "Sure," he said and walked out of the room together with the nurse so that Max could change. As soon as they were alone, Max relaxed.

"Martha what happened?" he asked.

"You collapsed at the fight sir," Martha begun at once. "The casino called an ambulance and the mayor called me. They had already brought you here to this hospital by the time I could get here. I called Dr. Benson and he arrived to check on you but they only allowed him in as a professional courtesy but they said he could not treat you because of that affiliation thing. He said to call him as soon as you woke. I've already sent him a text."

"Good girl. Anything else?" Max asked.

Martha shook her head. "Everything is under control sir. Whitby is handling the press, Constantine has informed the board of what is happening."

"What's he telling the press?" Max wanted to know.

"No information at this time," Martha said.

Max nodded. "That might not be the best strategy for the stocks. Ask him to change that to a bad case of the flu."

"Yes sir," Martha said taking out her phone to text Whitby.

"Where is Andrea?" Max asked.

"She's taking care of canceling or rescheduling appointments sir. She should be here this afternoon."

"Right. Good." Max said.

"Also, your mother called," Martha said tentatively.

Max was silent, staring at the ceiling.

"She...wanted to know how serious it was," Martha said.

Max turned to look at her. "What did you tell her Martha?" he demanded.

Martha shrugged her ample shoulders. "I told her the doctors didn't know. She asked me to keep her informed."

Max's eyes narrowed and Martha hastened to add, "I said I would tell you to get in touch."

Max's brow cleared and he snorted, "She probably was hoping I'd cop it and she'd have a chance at inheriting everything."

"Yes sir," Martha said obediently.

Max looked around the room, his frown returning.

"I have some things for you in the car, your robe, slippers, laptop, some flowers to brighten the room and your throw rug for the floor," Martha said seeing the frown. Max nodded his approval.

"Great, bring them in. Especially the laptop," he said.

Martha nodded and left as Max lay back.

*****

"Hey gra, how are you?" Christine called as she heard her grandmother come in. She looked at the clock tick tick ticking away in the hall. Ten pm. Late even by her grandmother's standards. That Mr. Lestrange worked her too hard.

"I'm good how are you?" Martha replied.

"Wonderful. We got a new intern at work today. Eager to please, good looking...I hate him," Christine replied.

Martha laughed shaking her head. "What am I going to do with you Chris?"

"Stop calling me by a boy's name?" Christine asked. "Anyway, why are you home so late? Another dinner party?"

Martha stopped massaging her feet to look up at Christine in surprise. "Mr. Lestrange is in the hospital Chris, show some compassion."

"What? What happened?" Christine asked moving to help her grandmother with her other shoe.

"The doctors say its some kind of infection. I don't have the details. I'm not kin," Martha said.

Christine snorted, "You're as much kin as any that man has."

Martha did not disagree.

"So...? Is he gonna be okay or are you out of a job?"

Martha glared at her. "You are so unfeeling at times girl."

"I'm not...I just...I don't think Max appreciates you as much as he should," she said.

Martha smiled. "Girl you know nothing. Now go get me a cuppa tea and stop bitchin," she said making Christine laugh as she went.

*****

Strings had been pulled and Dr. Benson had been given a temporary pass to treat his patient Max Lestrange in the hospital. The tests were back and Dr. Schofield and Dr. Benson stood before him to explain the results.

"Your blood work showed elevated levels of white blood cells which would seem to indicate an infection. We did differential testing to narrow down the source of the infection and we're pretty sure it's some form of prostatitis. We still need to do further tests including a biopsy to narrow down the possibilities," Dr. Benson said.

"Biopsy...isn't that to find cancer?" Max asked concentrating on making his face impassive.

"Yes. It's just to cover all bases. You're thirty eight years old and that's still below the high risk age for prostate cancer but we can't ignore the possibility," Dr. Schofield replied.

Max studied them and then nodded. "Okay then...when?"

"Tomorrow morning," Dr. Schofield said.

"What does it entail?" Max asked tensing just a little bit.

"The procedure we're going to do is known as a trans-rectal biopsy," Dr. Benson said. "It means we'll be accessing your prostate through your rectum. The procedure will be done right in this room. A nurse will be by early to give you an enema."

"Enema?" Max repeated in horror.

"It's necessary," Dr. Benson replied.

Dr. Benson turned to the nurse motioning her forward. "Nurse Marcus here has a consent form for you to sign, feel free to read it over and if you have any questions I'm around."

"Thank you," Max said taking the form and trying to read. His vision was blurry however so he picked up his phone and hit speed dial two.

"Clarence? I need you to come tell me if I should sign this consent form or not," he said into the receiver.

"I'm at the administration wing facilitating your move to somewhere where we can control the environment better. I'll be there in ten minutes," Clarence said.

"Okay," Max said and hung up. There was movement at the door and he looked up to behold a fairly tall woman the color of café au lait, her honey eyes regarding him with cool curiosity. She'd tied her curly black hair in a pony tail with the ends exploding all over the place like a squirm of wriggling worms; only much better looking. Her cupid's bow mouth was pursed in disapproval like it always was when she looked at him. She had on some sort of dark lipstick and she was dressed for work in blue coveralls.

"Hey Chris," Max said.

Her frown got even worse. "Don't call me that," she said.

"Come to see if I'm dying?" Max asked with a mouth twist of his own.

"Oh you wish you were that important to me. Gra sent me to bring you lunch."

"Kind of you to go out of your way like this," Max said still in that baiting tone.

"Actually, there is a faulty transformer I need to look at nearby. The hospital is on my way. So you want your lunch or not?"

Max shrugged. "Hey, you're the one lurking in the doorway."

Christine stepped into the room proffering a small square bag. She placed it on the table and unzipped it, unloading a plate piled with greens and covered with transparent foil. She put the plate on his bed table and then extracted another plate arranged with fish fingers and baked potato. Lastly, there was a container of sauce.

"Looks good," Max said. "I don't suppose there's any wine in there."

Christine just glared at him and then extracted a bottle of sparkling water. "That's all you get," she said sternly.

Max pouted like a baby. "Why?" he wailed.

Christine just ignored him and turned to leave.

"Hey Chris?" Max said. Christine turned around to glare at him.

"Thanks for the delivery," he said.

Christine said nothing, just resumed her walk out of his room.

*****

The examination was not as horrible as Max imagined it would be, but the pain of having his intergluteal cleft penetrated was exacerbated by his mother calling his phone right after. Andrea, his personal assistant, usually fielded all calls from France just in case his mother was using someone else's phone but she wasn't here right now and Max had thought it was Martha...or Christine. So he hadn't glanced at the caller ID before picking up. His mind might have been on the throbbing sensation emanating from his ass and maybe worried about the fact that bleeding was said to be a possible side effect of the procedure.

"Max *mon cher,*" her mother's voice spread like a noxious cloud inside his head.

"*Maman*, what can I do for you?" Max replied.

"Je voulais juste voir comment vous faisiez *mon cherie*," Claire Lestrange said. She wasn't even French; she'd moved to France when she married Oscar Lestrange but she was originally from the Mid West. Max had gone to school in France, he'd spent only holidays in America until he joined Harvard University to pursue law and yet he didn't keep dropping French words into his conversations like his mother did. He found her to be an extremely pretentious twat. Perhaps because she was little better than white trash before her Oscar picked her up at a county fair one day and fancied himself in love with her. The honeymoon had lasted only long enough to produce one child and then Oscar and Claire Lestrange had gone their separate ways. Not too far though...Oscar wouldn't grant her full custody and Claire was not about to let go of that child support.

"I am doing well thank you for asking *Maman*, however I'm very tired and I need my rest so I will talk to you another time," he said hanging up before she could come up with the real reason for her call which probably involved some sob story about how she needed more money. Now that his father was dead, Max was in charge of his vast fortune in real estate and automotive parts. The latter had began as a passion of Oscar's and had grown into a multi million dollar enterprise with an exclusive Formula One contract. That was in addition to his own businesses in America that mostly consisted of making deals and getting in on the ground floor of profitable ventures. His investment in the Fast and Furious franchise for example had netted him a pretty penny plus his company provided the parts for all the cars.

He'd said he was tired just to get rid of his mother but Max found himself drifting off to sleep soon after that phone call. He guessed this...whatever it was...was really taking it out of him.

*****

"It might be cancer," Dr. Benson said looking solemn. "It might be just a severe case of prostatis. We have to be prepared-"

"Is it going to kill me Carlyle?" Max interrupted.

Dr. Benson sighed. "No. You're in excellent health and this type of cancer is curable. But we're jumping the gun here; the disease is not confirmed. The results of the biopsy are not out."

"What does the treatment entail?" Max asked ignoring the disclaimers.

"It varies from watching the situation to aggressive radiotherapy," Carlyle said.

"I vote for the latter," Max said at once.

"We have to wait for the results Max," Carlyle said with a tired sigh.

"What are the repercussions of treatment. Haven't I heard something about impotence?"

Carlyle took a seat and crossed his legs. "Yes, impotence is a possible side effect, as well as sterility. There are also other effects and hence why we need to be sure before we go further," he said sternly.

"Hey Carlyle, while we are waiting for results would it be possible for me to go home?" Max asked.

Dr. Benson thought about it. "I suppose Martha can watch over you just as well if not better than the nurses here. You cannot stay alone, she will have to board with you while you're invalid," he said.

Max rolled his eyes but nodded his acquiescence.

Chapter 2

Martha entered Max's room to bring in his laundry. It was early morning and he was still buried deep in the covers. Martha was relieved to see it. She'd left him pacing in his study when she finally gave up the ghost and retired to bed at 2am. Dr. Benson had said she should monitor him, make sure he got plenty of rest and enough to eat but there was only so much she could do. She could hardly order him to bed even though she was tempted to do just that last night. She knew he was worried about the disease he might have and what it might mean for his life. There was very little she could do about it except be around if he needed her.

She deposited his laundry in the closet and then returned to the kitchen to put the coffee on. Max still lived in the same apartment he'd acquired when he came to Boston to attend Harvard University. It was located in an old building between Fuller Avenue and Thorndike Street, in a Classical Revival apartment building which had five stories. The entrance is elegantly framed by paired and fluted Corinthian columns. Cast stone covers the walls of the first and second floors while the upper floors are faced with tan brick. Max's apartment was on the fifth floor and it spanned the entire length of the building so he was able to enjoy both sunlight and sunset through the huge bay windows. The East wing had a breakfast nook situated right next to the windows and that was where Martha set up his breakfast. The intercom went off and Martha hastened to answer before it awakened Max.

"Yes? Who is it?" she asked a bit curtly.

"Gra, its me," Christine said her voice sounding tinny and far away through the intercom. Martha pressed the button to let her in to the building and then called downstairs to the concierge to let her come up. She was waiting at the door when the elevator stopped at their floor.

"What's wrong?" she asked tensely.

Christine smiled. "Why do you think anything's wrong?" she asked walking into the spacious foyer and placing her coat on the priceless seventeenth century table like it was a fifty dollar coat rack. Martha moved to pick up the coat and hang it up in the closet near the door, there for just such a purpose.

"You don't just show up at my work unless there's a problem," Martha said turning around to face Christine.

"That's because you usually come home at night. I haven't seen you for two days," Christine said in a tone that could be construed as whining if one were being picky.

"You're a big girl Chris, you don't need to see me everyday," Martha said with a snort, leading the way to the kitchen.

"Usually grandmothers say the opposite thing," Christine replied and then putting on a high whiny soprano she continued. "You never call me; I don't see you anymore," she said before returning her voice to the normal tenor that it was. "That's what you're supposed to say."

"Well I see you a lot more than never; seeing as we live together so that would just be stupid wouldn't it?" she said opening the kitchen door and strolling toward the coffee pot. She didn't turn around to see if Christine was following.

"Christine," a deep voice called from down the hall.

Christine turned around to see Max walking toward her in his pajamas and the most comfortable pair of house slippers she'd ever seen. He was looking right at her as he walked and she paused to wait for him.

"Hello Max, you're looking better than the last time I saw you," she said coolly.

"Huh, so it was you who rang? I thought perhaps Andrea had gotten past the Gestapo at the gate and gained entry," he glanced at Martha as he said Gestapo.

"Nope, just lil ol' me," Christine said trailing in her grandmother's wake to the kitchen but not wanting to enter until Max took himself off somewhere else. She did not want to be caught in a three way discussion with her grandma's boss. That would just be awkward.

"How kind of you to come see how I'm doing," Max said.

Christine raised an eyebrow. "Now why would you think that's why I came?" she asked.

Max shrugged. "I don't know, I just figure that beneath all the veiled hostility is a heart that beats wildly for me," he grinned as he said it anticipating her ire. She just glared at him though, swirled past him and into the kitchen.

"Gra your charge has awoken," she declared knowing that Max had followed behind her.

"Good morning Max; are you ready for your breakfast?" Martha asked.

"Only if the pair of you will join me," Max said quite charmingly.

Martha was already nodding her agreement so Christine couldn't exactly tell him where he could put his invitation but only because she was very well bred.

They sat down to a fruity breakfast; after Max had consumed his customary cup of coffee, Martha handed him a vegetable smoothie to cleanse his palate. He grimaced over it and insisted that if he had to have one then so did Christine.

"How old are you? Five?" Christine snorted as her grandmother placed another smoothie firmly on her place mat.

"Isn't that how old you usually say I am anyway?" Max said with a grin. "Anyway, jokes aside I need to speak with you both and there is no time like the present."

Christine opened her mouth to point out that she was not his employee and therefore did not need to hear his directives or whatever but her grandmother narrowed her eyes at her and she shut her mouth.

"I might have prostate cancer," Max began and Christine's urge to be a nuisance instantly faded away. It was just a reflex anyway after all these years.

"I'm sorry," she said. Her grandmother said nothing.

"The doctors have advised me on treatment and my prognosis, which is fairly good. However after treatment I might end up sterile or impotent...maybe both," he said looking down at his smoothie.

"Ouch," Christine said.

"Yes, well I don't tell you this for your sympathy. Martha you know that I want children," he said. Martha nodded her head.

"Well that desire hasn't changed but my ability to have them soon might..." his voice trailed away uncertainly.

"What do you need from us?" Christine asked briskly.

"I grew up with the worst mother, both of you know that. I don't want to subject my child to that. But I also don't want to condemn them to having no mother at all."

"Uh huh?" Christine said brow furrowing in confusion. She could see why Max had wanted to talk this over with Martha, after all, she'd literally been the only mother figure he'd ever known. But why her?

"I also...well finding the right surrogate in my position is not an easy thing but last night I thought about something which I wanted to run by you," Max was looking at Christine as he said this and she did not know why.

"Go ahead," she said.

"Will you carry my child?" he asked.

Christine dropped her glass of smoothie...although that might not totally have been by accident.

"What?" she asked.

"Hear me out," Max said hands spread placatingly.

"I am," Christine replied calmly.

Max opened his mouth, and then closed it again. He took a deep breath and started again, "You and Rudy-"

"Don't talk about Rudy," Christine cut in curtly.

"Okay then, all I meant to say was that I know that he hurt you badly and you haven't gotten involved with anyone else since," he hastened to speak as she opened her mouth to protest. "I'm just saying that you...and I are *both* damaged goods; we're both protecting ourselves from hurt and disappointment but we both want to have a family. I know you do because you told me."

"What has this got to do with-" Christine bit out, her face thunderous and glowing with emotion.

"You could have a child, with me. I'm not asking for happily ever after here. I'm just saying this is one dream we both have that we could fulfill for each other."

"You've lost your mind," Christine said, glancing at her oddly quiet grandmother, surprised that she hadn't jumped in here.

"No I haven't. But I *will* lose my ability to have children pretty soon," he said.

"You don't know that. You're not even sure it's cancer," Christine protested.

"Am I going to wait until they put the results in my hand and tell me we have to go into surgery fast before I do what needs to be done? What if there is no time after they find out what's wrong? I gotta do this while the getting's good otherwise I might not have another chance."

"But what if it turns out that what you have is perfectly treatable and curable without taking away your ability to have children? What then?"

"I still want to have kids. I *know* you'll make a good mother simply because your grandmother is a great mother. I'd still want it to be you."

"But what if I don't want to be the mother of your children?" Christine asked. There was a lump in her throat that she didn't know why it was there.

"Rudy is no longer available Chris," Max said, a tad cruelly in Christine's opinion.

"Don't call me that," she said.

"Will you at least think about it?" he asked.

Christine sighed and looked at her grandmother, waiting for some clue as to how to proceed. Her grandma looked impassively back, leaving the decision entirely to her.

"I will try to think about," she said at last.

"Thank you Christine," Max said standing up to leave the table. He bent forward and planted a kiss on her cheek and then went around the table to do the same for her grandma. Christine was royally confused.

*****

"So you're just going to sit there and not say anything?" she asked her grandma when Max's footsteps had stopped echoing in the hallway. He must have reached his bedroom.

Martha shrugged, "You know I try not to come between you kids. Your fights are always too brutal for me."

"This isn't a fight and we're not kids. What Max is suggesting is far from kiddish...even if it *is* to do with kids. And it's madness. You know this. Why didn't you speak up? He'd have listened to you," Christine said chidingly.

Martha studied her. "If you think that, why didn't you just say no?" she asked impassively.

Christine widened her eyes at her, "Are you kidding me? Of course I didn't say no. He could have cancer!" she exclaimed.

"Yes. But whether or not that is true, if you think that the idea is madness then you should shoot it down. You say you're not kids, but you still want your gra to tell you what to do..."

"That is not fair," Christine frowned at her.

"You can't have your cake and eat it Chris; either this is madness in which case you need to shut it down, or else it's an idea worth considering in which case it's your decision."

Christine glared at her. "I really hate that you're so wise," she grumbled.

Martha smiled and stood up to head back to the kitchen. "I'll pack you a nice lunch. Why don't you head to the sunroom, its gorgeous this time of day. Perfect for thinking," she said.

Christine made a face at her behind her back but then stood, went to the side board to pour herself some coffee and then headed to the sunroom to think.

* * * * *

She thought about her relationship with Rudy; they had met on the first day of college at MIT; they were the only two black students in the Electrical Engineering Freshman class and so they naturally gravitated toward each other. The stress of college and their natural competitiveness might have torn them apart instead it made them closer. Unlike Christine's humble roots however, Rudy came from a well off New York family who, if not outwardly hostile, were still ambivalent about having her in his life. Christine had hoped that once they got to know her...especially after Rudy *proposed,* that they would soften up.

It was Max who had dropped the truth bombs on her. He'd told her that they would never accept her, that she would never be good enough for the likes of them, that Rudy would break her heart... she'd hated him for it. And hated him even more when every one of his predictions came true. Rudy left her at the altar for a white woman. He hadn't so much as tried to fight for her against his family. Christine had wanted to stay and fight but Max had whisked her off to an island on the Caribbean with her grandmother. They kept her there for three weeks, plying her with alcohol and good advice; trying to get her over the bump. All she'd wanted to do was leave, to run to New York and Rudy; to make him see that they were meant to be. But there was no way off the island except Max's private plane – and that was not available to her until Max said so. She had cried and pleaded and begged but neither Max nor her grandmother listened to her. They just plied her with more drinks and more soothing words while she felt like she might go crazy if she didn't *move*.

Once the turmoil in her head calmed down a little though, she decided that the best strategy to ensure she got off the island was to pretend to be better. She tried to smile; she toasted to her Rudy-free future, she audibly made plans to move on. The more she did these things, the more relaxed Max and her grandmother became. After a week of visibly relaxing she said she should get back. She had her last semester of college to attend and she needed to prepare for that. Rudy would still be in her class; she would have to deal with that and not let it affect her grades. She'd worked too hard to achieve her dreams to let this little snafu trip her up. Martha and Max cheered her on, promised they would do anything they could to make life better. Max even offered to get Rudy expelled...though she was eighty per cent sure that had been a joke.

They left the island that week and once they got back Christine made no sudden moves, just got on with the business of returning gifts – even though her grandmother offered to do it – and writing thank you notes to anyone who had been of help to her or sent her a gift. Once she was through with that, she made preparations to go back to school. It was her last semester and most of the work was done. Her project was almost complete and she was on the fast track to graduating as an electrical engineer. Rudy would not be able to avoid her in school; she would make him see the error of his ways. Christine was still young at the time, only twenty three; she'd thought there was a chance for them. In spite of everything he'd done to her, she still thought she could turn things around.

That hadn't been the worst thing to happen to her though...

She bought some new clothes and put in a long 'Asian hair' weave and revamped her look. She did her best to look the way Rudy's mother and sister did; sophisticated, svelte and sexy. She took a dance class because she'd heard dancing made one move more gracefully. She wanted every weapon in her arsenal that she could get.

When the semester began she kept clear of Rudy, as far away from him as possible in fact. He didn't try to talk to her or even explain himself even though she hadn't seen him since the aborted wedding ceremony when Max and her grandmother had whisked her out of there so fast her head had spun. Maybe if they'd given him more time, he would have…

The semester wasn't too hard, most of the work was done; Christine was mostly on autopilot but she was getting by. And then there was a test, and a book of Rudy's that she still had — and he wanted it back. So he came to her room to get it; the room she'd *insisted* on getting despite 'suggestions' from both her grandmother and Max that she stay off campus. Max even went so far as to offer her transportation to school if she continued to stay at home. She'd pushed the offer back at him as rudely as she could, reminding him that he was *not* nor had ever been the boss of her, let alone her father. He'd back off which was great, but he'd also looked hurt; which she did not understand *at all.*

Rudy ended up spending the night with her, she'd played hard to get for a bit but she couldn't lie. She wanted him back so she was so glad to have him back in her bed, desperate for her, making noises that let her know he wanted her. She wanted him right back and she was so happy he'd come back to his senses. In the morning when she woke up, he was gone.

She'd cried into her coffee that morning, skipped class and went for a boat ride on the river, letting the breeze play on her face and just tried not to think too hard. She went back to class the next day and acted like everything was fine and when Rudy knocked on her door two nights later, three sheets to the wind and begging to come in... she let him in. This time he was still there in the morning but in hindsight Christine figured it was because he passed out. She had to leave him there eventually with a note telling him there was coffee in the coffee maker and muffins under the basket since she had class. He staggered into afternoon class looking miserable but didn't make any particular effort to interact with her. A week later he banged on her door at 2am and this time Christine tried to talk to him, have a conversation. He apologized to her, at long last, about what happened at the wedding. He explained that his family was partial to Natasha because they'd been like peas in a pod since they were very young and it was *understood* by both families that they would eventually wed. It was unfortunate that she'd chosen to interrupt their wedding like that but there was really very little that Rudy could do about it at the time and Christine had seemed to be okay. She'd left with her grandmother and her grandmother's boss as if she was fine with it anyway and Rudy had tried texting her but there was no reply.

Christine explained that Martha had confiscated her phone and that was why she hadn't answered. He asked that they continue as they were, seeing each other in secret for now until Rudy could resolve things with his family. Christine readily agreed; she didn't think her grandmother would want to know about her rekindled romance with Rudy and her friends certainly wouldn't understand that he was the love of her life. When Christmas break rolled around he had gone to his family in New York and she had stayed in Massachusetts with her mother and her grandmother. The day after Christmas she was taking a break from the mayhem and chaos that was Christmas holidays at her grandmother's to surf the net and catch up on entertainment news. She was addicted to tabloids. After she was all caught up on what Beyonce was doing, she decided to google Rudy...just to see what would come up.

What came up was his application for a marriage license for Rudy Sinclair and Natasha McCann. Christine stared at it in shock and then shook her head, looking up the picture matching the social security number listed. It was Rudy alright...*her* Rudy. The one who had fucked the hell out of her the night before he left town and assured her that he would miss her and wished he didn't have to leave. *That* Rudy...

There was nobody she could tell; nobody she could whine to or complain to. She was supposed to be over him; everyone assumed she was over him.

She had gone over to Max's place with her grandmother the next day. He always had the good alcohol and had no objection to her sampling it as long as her grandmother didn't mind. Martha had been fine with her drinking alcohol as soon as she turned 21 so that was no longer an issue. As soon as Martha let them into the apartment she headed straight for the library that had the most well stocked bar. The living room bar was okay but the good stuff was in Max's private library stash. She picked up a bottle which said 'Legacy by Angostura' which looked like a likely candidate to get her drunk really fast. Plus it was rum, which she liked unlike most other types of alcohol. She sat down in Max's chair and poured herself a glass.

Chapter 3

The wine was a lot more potent than she'd imagined. She'd only finished one glass before she started to feel woozy. When Max found her there, she'd had three glasses and was an angry drunk.

"Christine!" he had exclaimed. "I didn't know you were in here."

Christine glared at him. "S'all your fault," she mumbled.

"What?" he asked.

"S'your fault. You did this to me," she complained, eyes drooping as she studied Max. He was a tall dude, really tall; maybe six two. And people considered him to be good looking...it wasn't just the money even. There was his dark hair and his dark eyes and his inherent *Frenchiness* that just made him seem elegant all the time even when his tie was askew and his shirt was untucked like now. Plus he carried himself like a stalking panther, all loping grace and power. Those wide shoulders of his looked like they could take the weight of the world on them.

"You're drunk," he said pointing out the obvious.

"No shit," she replied managing to sound sarcastic even though she was slurring her words pretty bad.

"What's wrong? You never get drunk," he said.

"How would you know?" she jeered at him.

"I know you," he countered which sounded like utter bullshit to her.

"If you know me so well then what am I thinking right at this moment?" she asked.

Max stared at her for a long while. "I don't know that anything you're thinking would be good for you in any way so I suggest that *instead* I help you to one of the guest rooms so you can get some sleep," he said.

"What? You're not going to call my gra? Let her know what a bad girl I'm being?" she asked.

"No, I'm not calling your grandmother because she doesn't need this shit. She works really hard to provide for you and she doesn't need to be worrying about where your head is right now. So you're going to sleep it off, whatever it is and tomorrow you go home and you make better decisions."

It was Christine's turn to study him for a long while. "You know," she declared.

"I know," he said.

"How?" she asked.

Max smiled. "You recovered too fast. You were too in love with him to be over him so completely the way you were pretending to be. And lately you've been happier again...glowing like you had a secret. Today that glow is gone, so I'm guessing you found the marriage license."

"You are pretty scary you know that?" she said cheeks flaming in embarrassment at being caught so completely.

"I know. It's a gift," he said with a smile. He came forward and wrapped his hand around her arm, pulling her out of his chair like that. She went along only because she didn't have enough coordination to resist him effectively. He took her to the guest room opposite his room, stripped her to her panties and tucked her into bed. She was just too drunk to be embarrassed.

The next morning he woke her with coffee, bacon, sausage and scrambled eggs in bed. He didn't talk about the night before or about the fact that he'd seen her almost naked. Still, she couldn't get it out of her head. As he gathered the tray to return to the kitchen, she stopped his moving away with a hand on his arm.

"Why didn't you take me up on that offer last night?" she asked.

He sat back down on the bed. "I wasn't about to take advantage of my housekeeper's granddaughter when she was drunk."

"So if I wasn't your housekeeper's granddaughter you *would* have taken advantage of me?" she teased.

Max shrugged. "I might have considered it...if we weren't in my house and you didn't know where I live," he said with a smile.

"Wow, sleazy much?" she said unimpressed.

"Hey, don't hate the player, hate the game," Max said.

Christine laughed. "That is so two thousand and late."

"Poetic," Max replied with a smile.

"So, I'm sober this morning. You wanna?" she said.

"Wow Chris, you are just soo romantic," he said.

"This isn't romance. This is a revenge fuck against my bastard of an ex fiancé who played with my heart, stomped on it, and set it on fire," she said.

"He won't even know," he protested.

"We could make a sex tape," she offered.

It was Max's turn to laugh, "No thanks."

"No thanks to the sex tape or…?" she persisted.

"You really want to?" he asked.

"Yes I really do," she replied.

"Really why?" he asked.

"Because I need a reboot. Rudy was my first, my only. I need to know that there is life after Rudy Sinclair. And I know you have the experience to show me that."

"I'm flattered."

"Will you do it?"

"Your grandmother can never know," he warned.

"Goes without saying."

"Okay then. You're not going to make me take you to dinner first?"

"Nope. None o' that shit. This is strictly a hit it and quit it situation."

"Every man's dream."

"Exactly."

*****

To Christine's surprise, Max did not jump her on the spot. He simply took her tray to the kitchen and then came back to her room, taking his place on the side of her bed again. They talked about work; they both had backgrounds in engineering so they were able to get technical about their shared interests. Christine found that she was getting more and more relaxed and before she realized it, Max had slung his arm around her shoulder and she was leaning into him.

"I'm so miserable," she said after a brief lull in the conversation.

"I'll make it better," he said kissing her forehead. His hand was softly caressing her arm. His other arm reached out to cup her chin and pull it up so he could rest his lips on hers. He began to bite along her jaw gently as she sat still and let him have his way with her. His other hand continued to caress her arm and her lips fell open, waiting for him to get to them. Of their own volition, her eyes slipped closed and her heart sped up.

"Tell me what you want," Max murmured against her skin.

"I want you to fuck me," Christine said succinctly. This caused Max to huff a laugh against her skin setting off tiny shivers to shimmer all over her skin.

"Do that again," she whispered. Max leaned closer and thrust his tongue in her ear. This time she couldn't hold back a scream in addition to her shivers. It could have been due to the cold wetness of his tongue or the sensations it was eliciting in her ear. She hooked her naked leg over his and his hand came down to run slowly down her thigh and then back up. His tongue traced the lines of her face before inserting itself into her mouth and proceeding to taste her. Christine leaned her whole body toward him asking mutely for his touch.

It was the signal he was waiting for apparently because in the blink of an eye, Christine was lying flat on the bed and Max was pressing down on top of her, sucking frantically at her neck. She lifted her arms tentatively and wrapped them around his neck, with her legs going around his waist almost in a mirrored gesture. Her pink panties were wet and Max's finger, rubbing gently along her gluteal cleft all the way around to her vaginal opening was not helping. The rub of the pink cotton against her skin seemed to add an extra dimension to the sensations shooting through her and she wriggled her behind, trying to get him to *do something*. He moaned softly into her neck and thrust forward; the hard bulge in his pajama pants rubbing against her already sensitized skin and driving her up the wall.

"Now now now now Max," she groaned in frustration.

"You are so impatient," he said laughing in her ear. Her only response was to arch upwards so that her covered vagina could rub against his hardness.

"Alright alright, jeez," he said reaching into his pajamas and palming his penis before pulling it out and pressing it against her cotton undies, driving her around the bend. He pressed forward into her, not bothering to get her panties out of the way and it was the most erotic thing that had ever happened to Christine. She felt him begin to penetrate her, her underwear getting pushed to the side by the simple expedient of having this large round object shoved into her. and Max was *very* large; she had known about it but hadn't believed that this size was actually real. She felt so filled that she was afraid for a second.

"Shh, I won't hurt you," Max whispered in her ear as if he could divine her thoughts. Curiously enough, his reassurances calmed her down, and she relaxed; letting him as deep inside her as he could go.

"Oh my God," she groaned.

"Close but no cigar. Its just me, Max," Max whispered in her ear.

"Har har de har har," she replied even though she could practically feel her kidneys shifting location to make room for him.

Suddenly he withdrew from her completely and thrust into her again, sheathing him to the hilt. She let out a gasp of equal parts surprise and arousal but he didn't give her time to recover before doing it again. Her legs spread wider of their own accord and she arched her back, letting him in as deep as he wanted to go. He wanted to go deep. Christine was afraid she might never walk again if things went on much longer.

"Please," she whispered not really knowing what she was pleading for. His tongue was in her ear again and she shivered.

"Tell me what you want," he said again. Christine's head was spinning. Rudy never asked her what she wanted…he just gave her what she needed; she guessed. She wrapped herself tighter around Max and rubbed her breasts against him, wanting to feel him everywhere. Her fingers were tingling with little shocks like she'd been electrocuted. Her toes were curled. If she could see it, she was sure her hair was standing on end. The electric shocks were striping through her at seemingly greater speed and velocity, the epicenter being the heat at the junction of her legs. She felt like she might die from it; she needed it to stop. She needed it to never stop. Her mouth opened and unintelligible words fell out; this followed by low key screaming. She needed to release this energy somehow because it seemed to be circling her body, causing chaos and confusion everywhere it touched down.

"Max," his name was punched from her throat in her agony of feeling. She needed this expanding feeling to contract or explode and she knew he was the key but didn't have the words to explain. He seemed to understand though because his rhythm sharpened and quickened, breath escaping from his body like a runaway steam engine, his hips jerking faster and faster into her, building up the heat, setting it up for a conflagration that would likely consume them both. Christine let him, lying back pliant, and heavy limbed awaiting the inevitable explosion. When it came it still took her by surprise with how it lifted her off the bed and contorted her body and then let her go so she felt it as her whole being liquefied and for a moment she understood what it means to be one with the universe.

They never did it again. They don't even talk about it. It's like it never happened.

*****

And now Max wants her to have his baby. What the hell is she supposed to do with that?

There is a tentative knock on the curved wall that separates the sunroom from the long hallway.

"What?" she asked not looking but knowing that it's Max.

"I wanted to see if maybe you have questions," he said.

Christine laughed bitterly, "Where to start?"

Max walked into the room and sat down tentatively opposite her, settling himself in the chair as if he was as uncomfortable as she was.

"Well let me ask a question then," he said. "Do you want to have a baby of your own?"

"You know I do," her answer was cold.

"Its been five years since you and Rudy broke up; you haven't had another steady relationship since," he began

"Don't you-" Christine began to snarl but Max put up his hand in a 'hear me out' gesture.

"All I'm saying is you seem to not want to put yourself in a situation to get hurt again; but you want kids. I'm offering you the opportunity to bring that dream to reality in a risk free way."

"How is this risk free?" Christine asked incredulously.

"You don't love me, therefore I can't break your heart. We both want the same thing; a child, so we're united in purpose. I know you're not just out for what you can get; you know you can trust me."

"I can trust you?" Christine repeated somewhat skeptically.

"You know you can," Max repeated.

Christine thought about this; if one disregarded the fact that it was a *totally crazy idea* it did kind of make perfect sense. After all it wasn't like she was holding out for Mr. Right here. He'd come, broken her heart, stomped on it, and gone. So Mr. Common Purpose might do just fine. And at least she knew she wouldn't have to go chasing him for child support or worry that he'd be a dead beat dad. Even if he turned out to have cancer, the prognosis was good so he was also unlikely to die on them. Plus gra didn't seem to have a huge objection to this so...

"We'd need a contract or something," she said and saw him relax into his seat. She hadn't realized how tense he was.

"Of course," he said.

"How are you going to explain this to your board of directors or whoever?" she asked.

"Hey, they run my company not my life."

"Okay then. When do you want to do this?" she said quite calmly considering she was *freaking out.* They were talking about having a baby together.

"I thought I could make a doctor's appointment for later today since you're on board. The sooner the better right?"

"I guess," she said thoughtfully. "So we're going the artificial insemination route?"

Max shrugged. "Unless you want-", he began.

"No," Christine cut in quickly. "Turkey baster is just fine. No need to blur the lines."

"Right so...lawyers first and then doctors," he said.

"Right."

*****

Clarence was just not getting it. "You want to do *what*?" he asked for the third time like he hadn't been accepted to Harvard Law School due to his reMaxable powers of deductive reasoning and getting the point pretty quickly.

"Christine and I would like to have a baby together," Max explained again, slowly, while Christine picked at a loose thread on her skirt.

"Where is this coming from?" Clarence asked again, darting a suspicious glance at Christine as she continued to play with her clothes and thus did not see his look.

"It's coming from the fact that I may not be able to have children after next week," he said.

"Because of the treatment?" Clarence said showing that he did in fact have the power of hearing.

"Yes," Max said pleased to have gotten that over with. "So we need a contract."

"I don't actually have one ready made lying around here. We don't usually deal with surrogacy," he said.

"This isn't really that because we'll both have rights to the child," Max clarified seeing as Christine had looked up at the word 'surrogacy' with a frown.

"Yes, so of course it's more of a contractual agreement to have a child together and raise it..." Clarence's voice trailed off helplessly.

"Exactly," Max said nodding.

"Right, well...I'll get my team on it and you should have copies sent to you by tomorrow morning."

"Great. Wonderful. That's why I pay those astronomic retainer fees of yours Clarence. You always come through."

Clarence just nodded miserably and ushered them out of the office.

* * * * *

The doctor's appointment didn't go much better. They had managed to squeeze in a fifteen minute preliminary session at the foremost fertility clinic in Boston which was just enough time for explanations and scheduling of tests. The doctor was of the opinion that they should wait for the results of Max's tests before taking such a drastic step but Max was adamant and Christine was silently supportive so there was no more to be said. Except to find out about Christine's reproductive history and when exactly her last period had been, whether she was on birth control and other stories. Max was instructed to leave a sperm sample as well so as to test his viability and after the extensive invasion of privacy and personal space that the test entailed Max and Christine were ready to call it a day.

"Ice cream?" Max asked as they drove in his Bentley back to his apartment.

"Some rocky road would go down real smooth right now," she agreed.

"Great," he said as he swerved into a side road that led to a tiny ice cream shop that Christine herself had brought him to, to drown his loneliness, when he first moved to Boston all those years ago. She'd been ten at the time and a foremost expert on names, locations and rankings of every single ice-cream shop in the vicinity.

They got some giant cones to go, feeling slightly better about their day.

"You remember the first time you brought me here? Good times," Max said between licks.

"Yep. Those were the good ol' days. When did life get so complicated?" she complained.

"Adulthood. Who needs it right?"

"Yeah," Christine agreed nostalgically. "Childhood is the best."

"They say that children bring back your own childhood," Max pointed out.

"Nice segueway there," Christine replied grinning. "I'm actually feeling...a bit excited about this."

"Yeah...me too," Max said. "I mean if there is anyone in the world I'd rather share a baby with it'd be you...okay actually it'd be Martha but that'd be too weird and crazy so you're the closest substitute."

"You just want your kid to be related to her," she accused.

Max shrugged. "Guilty as charged."

Christine's head came up and her eyes widened. "Have you told your mom about this?" she asked. "Oh my God I forgot my child would be related to her as well."

"Hey!" Max protested.

"What? You're the only one allowed to talk shit about her?"

"Yes."

"Okay fine. Fair enough. Sorry. But have you told her?"

"There's no need for her to know. She'd just do her level best to stop it and I don't feel like dealing with her shit on top of all the other shit in my life right now."

Christine studied him with a frown. "You're really scared."

Max shrugged. "I'm terrified. My dad died of cancer you know."

"I know...but it was liver cancer; its non-genetic and probably something to do with all the drinking he did," Christine said then grimaced. "Sorry."

"No...it's fine. My parents were/are a hot mess."

Christine shrugged. "Whose parents aren't? My mother is on her fourth marriage to yet another dead beat and my father is God knows where. For all I know he's dead."

"Yeah but your grandmother's great."

"That is true."

Max smiled over at her. "I'm glad we get to share her."

"Aha. The ulterior motives come out," Christine solemnly said.

Chapter 4

Max's sperm tests went swimmingly and his seed was given a seal of good health. Christine was found to be healthy and fertile with a uterus that was ready to carry a child to term. All that was left was for her ovulation to take place which was serendipitously imminent.

"Let's do this then," Max told the doctor eagerly. "I'm told you can determine the sex by when the sperm is introduced in the vagina?"

"There are some old wives' tales to that effect," Dr. Mulholland stated as he prepared Christine for insemination.

"Any truth to it?" Max persisted.

"Some," the doctor said in a preoccupied tone. "Why you have a preference?"

"I don't know. A daughter would be nice; but stressful. I don't know if I could stand by and watch her go on dates when she achieves adolescence. Boys are great too; we could do a lot of stuff together…I'm torn can we have one of each?" he grinned at Christine who glared back.

"Yeah lets do that. You carry one and I'll carry the other."

"Alright then...lets stick with one."

"That's what I thought," Christine said with a snort.

Max just smiled at her.

Once the procedure was done, Christine was required to lay on the bed with her feet up for an hour. Max and Martha waited outside for her to be done, not talking much.

"Are you scared?" Martha asked at some point.

"No," Max replied.

"Liar."

Max smiled, "I don't think you're supposed to speak that way to your boss."

"I think that ship has sailed," Martha commented with a side smile.

Max sighed. "Thank God. I'm not much of an employer anyway."

"Is this national bullshit day or something?" Martha said.

Max laughed, "I love you Martha."

Martha just snorted.

*****

"It's not cancer," Dr. Benson informed him two weeks later. "What you have is something called CPPS. The symptoms are similar and so are the tests and so it's easy to confuse. But the biopsy results finally came through and you do not have malignant tissue."

"What is CPPS? What's my prognosis?" he asked not sure if he should be relieved.

"Chronic prostatitis typically causes pain in the lower pelvic region of men. Urinary symptoms such as frequency of passing urine and pain on passing urine may also be present. Treatment can be difficult and may include antibiotics and other drugs. Symptoms may last a long time, although they may 'come and go' or vary in severity," Dr. Schofield recited as if he'd memorized it.

"Great, so I can expect pain...and resurgence of symptoms. Am I going to be fainting all over the place from now on?" Max asked.

www.SaucyRomanceBooks.com/RomanceBooks

"Not really. But there are of life issues to be considered. The possibility of developing autoimmune disorders, systemic inflammation...every case is different; so planning a course of treatment is dependent on your symptos. Right now you have a slight inflammation in your right kidney that we'll treat with intravenous antibiotics. We require you to stay overnight in the hospital. It will be painful but we can manage you better here. It would be better if you weren't alone..." Dr. Benson's voice trailed away uncertainly. He was aware that Max had no family in Boston. Max said nothing for a long while.

"How long will I be out of commission?" he asked at last.

"A few days. Maybe a week," Carlyle said.

Max just lay back and closed his eyes. The doctor left him alone.

*****

A soft knock woke him from a pain fueled dream a few hours or minutes later. He wasn't sure. He opened his eyes slowly, mainly because it hurt to move any muscle in his body. The doctors hadn't been exaggerating the level of pain. If his brain was in any position to measure, he was sure his pain would be about a 20 on a scale of one to ten. He tried to focus on who was at the door but all he saw was a blur. A café au lait blur, about five ten, big hair...Christine.

"Hey," he said scratchily.

"Hey. I don't know if it's too weird being here but Gra's arthritis is acting up and she didn't think she could spend the night in this hard uncomfortable hospital chair-"

"I wouldn't ask her to," Max interrupted even though talking caused him severe pain.

"Of course you wouldn't but she knows that you need her. so she asked if I would mind..." Christine finished with a shrug.

"You don't have to do this," he forced out.

"I know I don't have to. But I already took the day off tomorrow so I kind of have to."

Max smiled painfully, turning his hand around so his palm was facing up. Christine looked down at it and then up at him. She put her palm gently atop his.

*****

Christine missed her period two weeks later but decided to keep it to herself until she could do a pregnancy test. She was really busy at work though, completing an electrification project on the north side of town which involved upgrading all the systems to reduce the risk of electrical mishaps taking place especially as winter was coming up and people used electricity for heating purposes. Her grandmother's arthritis was also a problem and the fact that she refused to slow down meant that Christine tried to take the brunt of household duties away from her. It involved driving her to work instead of letting her take the train like she enjoyed doing. She was also doing the cooking because her gra hated take out. Max had hired additional help at the house on the pretext that with is new invalid status, there was just a lot more to be done. The number of visitors at the house had also increased drastically since the whole state of Boston seemed to feel it was their duty to visit Max in his time of illness.

Eventually, Max was out of bed and at full strength and the flare up of arthritis was relieved. The project was still at full throttle though, so Christine still had a reason to put that doctor's appointment off.

She was on top of a ladder tinkering with a transformer when someone called her name on the walkie talkie.

"What?" she asked irritably; she wasn't one for interruptions.

"Wow, irritable much?" the voice crackled from the speaker.

"Max?" she said in disbelief.

"Yeah. Could you come down here? I need to talk to you."

"Should you be out of bed?"

"Oh now you care?"

"What's that supposed to mean?"

"I haven't seen you since the night you spent with me at the hospital. Now you're concerned that I'm out of bed?"

Christine sighed in exasperation, "I'm coming down."

"Great."

*****

"My turn to bring you lunch," he said as she approached him, holding out a paper bag.

"How sweet,", she said taking the bag and opening it. She peeked into the bag.

"It's a cheese and onion sandwich," Max said. But Christine could smell it already. She'd put her head in the bag and then took a deep breath so the deep fried smell of onion surrounded her like a toxic cloud. The wave of nausea it evoked took her completely by surprise. She thrust the bag back at Max and staggered to the river bank, breathing in and out deeply. The stench of the Charles had her staggering away as her empty stomach heaved.

"Oh," she thought she heard Max say.

A hand came out to hold her steady while another rubbed at her back as she heaved. A green rope of bile hung from her mouth and she spit it out. Max produced a bottle of water from somewhere and Christine drank; rinsing out her mouth.

"Are you okay?" Max asked.

"Do I *look* okay?" Christine replied irritably.

"You look like someone suffering from morning sickness."

Christine glared at him.

"That's unlikely," she said.

"Is it?" he asked eyebrow raised skeptically.

Christine said nothing.

"Right, so I'll make the appointment," Max said. "I'll come for you in the morning."

Christine nodded her head in agreement but continued to say nothing. Max stared at her assessingly, wondering if he could leave her alone.

"I'm just gonna go get you something less…noxious…to eat. Maybe an avocado sandwich? Or cucumber?" he asked.

"The latter," Christine said.

"Okay then, coming right up," Max said.

He walked off to find the nearest sandwich shop, heart beating at a rate that could not be accounted for by the walking. If it was true indeed that Christine was…with child…

Max cut off the thought before it could permeate his entire being and leave him shaking with how much he wanted it to be true. Still he found himself planning to stock his pantry with cucumber and water melon and other stink free vegetables.

*****

"You're pregnant," Dr. Mulholland said as if she didn't already know. On the seat next to her, Max slumped back as if in relief. Christine spared him a glance but her head was reeling with confusion. She could not really process anything.

"Well...what now?" she asked.

"Now...we dance," Max grinned.

*****

Christine was waiting when her grandmother got home that night, sitting in the kitchen alcove, a glass of milk at her elbow.

"You heard?" she asked.

"That I am to be a great grandmother? Yes," Martha said.

"Do you have any thoughts, feelings, reactions about it? Share with the class," Christine said.

Martha smiled. "Leave that aside for a moment; tell me how *you* feel."

"Me? I feel…confused, uncertain."

"But you knew this was a likely outcome when you had the doctor's appointment two weeks ago right?"

Christine shrugged. "I thought it would take more time than just once, in spite of your endless lectures," she said with a smile.

"Well I am proved right yet again. So what now?" Martha asked.

"We haven't even signed the contract yet," Christine said in a shaky voice.

"How come?" Martha asked.

"First Max was sick and then I was busy and then he didn't have cancer and I thought that the point was moot…now I'm pregnant."

"Well then I suggest the first order of business would be for you to talk to Max," Martha suggested.

*****

Martha got in to work a bit late the next morning due to the late night she'd had with Christine brainstorming on the next steps. Max was waiting for her in the foyer.

"Hi," he said.

"Hello Max. How are you feeling today?"

"Well enough to be worried about you. You're late. Is everything okay?"

"You mean is Christine okay," Martha said dryly.

"That too, yeah."

"Well you have her number. Why don't you call her and ask her?"

"I will. Thank you for the suggestion. Now, are *you* alright?"

"Yes Max, I'm fine. Living the dream," Martha was smiling, even humming a little as she deposited her handbag in the closet and took off her coat.

"That's great. I made you breakfast."

Martha turned to regard him in surprise, "Why?"

"Because I can...and I need to speak to you."

"Well, this is just...unfortunate because I just had breakfast at home. My doctor advised me to lose some weight because of the arthritis so I don't think I should eat again."

"Okay then will you have coffee with me?"

"Black, no sugar."

"Coming up. Go sit down and wait for me?"

"Alright," Martha said walking toward the breakfast nook. She picked up an apple from the fruit basket and bit into it as she awaited her coffee.

Max brought it, served on a tray in a mug with "World's Best Mom" on it. Martha regarded it in amusement.

"Where did you get this?" she asked.

"I bought it at a flea market yesterday. After I dropped Chris home I was...a bit restless so I went downtown and wandered about a bit thinking about her, me, my parents, her parents...and you. I just want to be the parent to my child that you have been to Chris."

"Don't put me on too high a pedestal. Have you met my daughter?"

"You blame yourself for that? At some point your kids grow up and they're responsible for their own decisions."

Martha was silent. "Well anyway, enough about me. What did you want to talk about?"

"I just wanted your input on the way forward."

"What do you have in mind?"

"Marriage," Max said.

"Marriage? I thought you wanted to be a co-parent. Where does marriage enter that equation?"

Max took a deep breath. "I'm not dying; I don't have cancer but that's about all that is certain. This thing that I have is of uncertain symptoms. I don't know what effects it's going to have on my body. This may well still be the only child I'm going to get. Even if it isn't the only child that I'm ever going to get, I owe it the chance to grow up with both parents."

"So you want to get married because the girl is pregnant? How many times has that worked out that you know of?"

"I don't want to get married because she's pregnant," Max said.

Martha grunted skeptically.

"What I mean is...I've known that girl since she was ten. I know who she is in a way that is different from the way I know other girls. I know her heart. I know that my heart would be safe with her."

"Your heart...? I thought this was a business arrangement?" Martha prompted.

Max was quiet for a bit. "It's not that cut and dried. It's not possible to have a child together and remain detached. Especially when the other person is already a friend. A good friend. Almost family. I'm just trying to be realistic about likely scenarios," he said.

"Have you talked to her about this?" Martha asked.

"I want to. It's difficult to find the words."

"And that's why you wanted to talk to me?"

"Exactly," Max replied.

*****

"Hello," Christine said answering her phone.

"Hey Chris. How are you?"

"I'm doing great. You?"

"Well, could use a good stiff drink but I understand I'm pregnant."

"*You're* pregnant? I thought *I* was pregnant."

"It's our baby, we're both pregnant."

"Aww, how sweet," Christine said sarcastically.

"So I wanted to find out if we could maybe talk?"

"Oh, you want to sign the papers and shit?"

"That...among other things. Will you meet me?"

"Yes of course," Christine said.

"Coffee at the Thinking Cup?"

"That is weirdly appropriate," she said.

"How's five o' clock work for ya?"

"Works just fine."

"Okay then, see you then."

*****

The coffee shop was full when Max drew up at exactly 5pm. He wondered if they would get seating but then spotted Christine sitting at a table reading something with a bag saving him a seat opposite her. He walked slowly toward her expecting her to look up at him but she continued to read. Max walked up to her and stopped right in front of her chair.

"Hey," he said making her jump. She really hadn't heard him coming...granted the bar was noisy but..

"You scared me," Christine said.

"Sorry," Max said moving to his seat and moving her bag to the table.

"No problem. What's shaking? You have the papers?" she asked holding out a hand for him to drop them into.

"Er...no. Clarence needs to get back to me on some specifics but I thought maybe we should talk about logistics, the way forward, how to handle this whole situation."

"Okay...but I thought all that would be in the contract?"

"Some things you can't legislate," Max said looking her in the eye, then his eyes dropped to the cup sitting in front of her. "What are you having?"

"Mocha cappuccino. Wanna taste?"

"No thank you, I'll just have an espresso if I can catch the eye of a waiter in this place. Wow it's loud here."

"Lots of people talking," Christine said with a shrug.

"Yeah, well anyway that Harry Potter character said it's the best way not to be overheard," he said, making her smirk.

"You are such a nerd," she said.

"So are you," he replied.

"Okay enough with the small talk. What's up?"

Max leaned back in his seat studying her intently. "How do you feel about a marriage of convenience?" he asked.

"You mean in general or...?" she asked with a raised eyebrow.

"I mean...would that be something you'd be interested in?"

"Why would I be?"

"Well, what if someone was offering?"

"Why would they offer?"

"Because maybe, the baby you're carrying might want to grow up with both parents."

"I thought he already was," the smirk was still on Christine's face.

"I meant together together. In the same house. It's not like you have anything else going on."

"Wow. That was my dream proposal. Hey Chris, how about it then? Not like you have anything else goin on," Christine said sarcasm dripping from every word.

Max smiled. "Hey, if I thought dinner and dancing in the moonlight would convince you I'd have gone that route. But I know you; you'd just think I was shining you."

"And you're not?"

"Why would I? To what end?"

Christine shrugged, "I don't know. Who knows why men do what they do?"

"Not you right? So why not take the safe bet? The man who won't break your heart and who happens to be the father of your kid as a bonus."

"As a bonus. Yay," Christine repeated.

"So is that a yes?"

"That is a 'I'm not sure what exactly is going on around here. I might need a few more conversations before I do' answer," she said fingering her teaspoon.

"Okay then, where would you like to have these conversations?"

Christine looked down and then glanced up at him from beneath her lashes. "I'm just sayin'...I think I rush into things and it gets me into trouble. Case in point...pregnant. I wanna do something different and take my time. Weigh my options. Find out what I'm getting into."

"If you were anyone else, I would describe to you the generosity of the prenup and turn your head with a diamond the size of your head. But since it's you, I don't know how to convince you that this would be a good idea. At least not without pushing some buttons I know would upset you."

Christine narrowed her eyes, "What buttons?"

Max took a deep breath, regarded her intently and then opened his mouth. "Did you enjoy growing up with an absent father?"

Christine's eyes narrowed further and Max hastened to jump in before she could say anything. "If you had a choice, wouldn't you have rather your mother and father living in the same house if they got along?”

Christine continued to glare, “We get along?”

Max shrugged, “More than most employer/housekeepers’ granddaughter combos I’ve seen.”

Christine laughed reluctantly, “Is that our frame of reference?”

“Hey, grading on a curve has got me through every day since kindergarten. I’m taking it,” Max said with a shrug.

“I…will think about it,” Christine said. “But so…does that mean no contract?”

“I thought we would combine the contract and the prenup if you’re amenable.”

“I think this is probably something you’d have to explain to your board of directors.”

“Again, they don’t run my life.”

“What about your mother?”

“She doesn’t run my life either.”

"I *mean* are you going to tell her?" Christine asked slowly as if he was retarded.

"Tell her what? You haven't given me an answer."

"What about the baby?"

"Plenty of time for her to hear the bad news."

"Bad news?"

"The fact that she's not my only heir?"

Christine lifted her brow, "Cynical much?"

"Realistic," Max said sipping on his coffee.

"Well anyway, this has been great and all but I have work tomorrow, I need to get my rest and there's traffic so I better get a move on."

"Yeah of course, let me pay the bill, I'll drop you off."

"I have my car thanks."

"Oh. Alrighty then. So I'll see you tomorrow?"

"Ye-es? See me for what?"

Max shrugged, "Just cause."

"So eloquent. I love it," she said with a smile.

Max smiled back but made no reply.

*****

She was eating dinner with her grandmother when something occurred to her.

"Oh my God, I have to tell mom about this don't I?" she asked her gra.

Martha shook her head, "Why do you have to?"

Christine shrugged, "I don't know. Maybe because she's about to be a grandmother?"

Martha smiled a bit cynically, "Forgive me but I don't think Cordelia is ready to be a grandmother just yet. That dead beat boy toy she's married to is definitely not ready to be a granddad."

"And they'd probably be out for what they can get too. Asking for loans and shit from Max?"

"You can probably count on that."

Chapter 5

Cordelia Richards walked into her house her eyes on the tabloid newspaper in her hands. There was a picture of her daughter having coffee with some rich guy. Cordelia was pretty sure it was the rich guy her mother worked for – it had been a while since she saw him but she was pretty sure he had a French name and so did this guy.

"Hmm, look what Chris is up to," she told her husband Kevin as she held the magazine out to him. He leaned forward to see the picture and read the caption.

"You think they fucking?" he asked her.

Cordelia shrugged, "Who knows. Maybe. Hhey, you think that's why Mama's kept that job so long. Because she was pimpin' Chris out?"

Kevin snorted, "Your mama be singin' in the choir every Sunday and shit...I don't think she's in the pimpin' game."

"So this Max guy just like dark meat then?" she asked peering at the picture of the guy.

"You talkin' bout your own daughter you know right?" Kevin said with a laugh.

"Oh I know. But look how they sittin. They lookin so cozy and shit. I bet they fuckin."

"Well then good for her right? He's loaded ain't he?"

"Pretty loaded. According to this article he's a billionaire."

"That's good right?"

Cordelia looked up from the article to stare at him. "You remember the last time she tried to hook up with a rich guy? My friends are still laughing at me," she said a tad bitterly.

"That's coz they jealous of your family doing well and all. Fuck em."

"Yeah well my 'family' may be doing well but I don't see no benefit from it. You'd think my darling professional engineer daughter might share the wealth but nooo...she pretty much ignores me."

"Yeah she a bit stuck up," Kevin agreed. "You want some weed?" he asked holding out a blunt.

"Yeah okay," she said putting aside the paper to take the blunt.

www.SaucyRomanceBooks.com/RomanceBooks

* * * * *

"Good morning Martha," Max said as she came through the front door. He was waiting in the foyer again, looking hopefully over her shoulder like he was waiting for someone else to come through.

"Good morning sir. Are we expecting company for breakfast?" Martha asked with a twinkle in her eye.

"I don't know. You tell me."

"Well as far as I know the answer is no. But perhaps Andrea can confirm that for you."

"God, you're such a pain sometimes Martha. Tell me how Chris is."

"Chris is fine. She left for work at 5am; something to do with a major power outage downtown. You should know if you're headed to your office."

"We have back up power so...anyway, so she's at work huh? Did she have breakfast before she left? Isn't that a bit early? Did she throw up?"

"Yes, yes, yes and yes," Martha said.

"Wow, does she need anything? Do we need to make an appointment with the doctor?"

"Have you chosen an obstetrician yet or is it the fertility doctor who will take you through?"

"Yeah, Dr. Mulholland will be taking us through."

"Great, so when is your next appointment?"

"Next Thursday, I think. That last meeting is kind of a blur in my mind, I don't think I heard anything after the doctor said 'You're pregnant'."

Martha smiled, "I don't blame you; it's shocking news even when you're expecting it. Topped with everything else that's been going on with you I'm guessing your body just wanted to shut everything down for a minute."

"Yes. Exactly. That's why I love talking to you. You always know exactly what I mean."

"Then maybe she's the one you should be making marriage proposals to," a voice said in the doorway making Max jump.

"Chris! I...didn't see you there."

"No shit," she replied with a shit eating grin.

"What are you doing here?" Max asked and then almost bit his tongue. "I mean...not that I *don't* want you to be here."

Christine waved a dismissive finger at him. "There was an accident at the site; I was told to go home for the rest of the day and I thought I'd come here and see my grandmother."

"Because you don't see me enough at home," Martha said dryly.

"Actually, I don't but also I need to discuss something with you... *privately,*" Christine said darting a glance at Max.

"And it couldn't wait until-" Martha began to say.

"No it couldn't," Christine replied curtly still darting glances at Max as if hoping he'd take the hint and just leave.

"Well, I'll leave you two to talk," he said at last, getting it.

Christine watched until he left the room and then lifted her shirt to show her grandmother a bruise on her pelvis.

"I fell," she said, mouth pouting exactly the same as when she was eight years old and wanted her grandmother to kiss away her boo boos.

Martha walked closer to examine the bruising. "Hmm, looks like it's swelling," she touched it gently and Christine flinched. "What happened?"

"I was on top of a ladder, there was a short circuit and the line that I was working on shot sparks in the air. It startled me and I kind of jerked backwards because I didn't want the sparks to hurt the baby. Then I fell, but Jermaine caught me so I didn't hurt myself too bad but my hip banged into the aluminum siding. Should I go to the hospital? Will the baby be hurt?"

Martha was still intently examining the site of injury. "Do you have any pain? Bleeding? Cramping?" she asked Christine pausing after each question for Chris' head shake.

"Well, usually if the baby is hurt then one of those things happens. However lets not take chances with my great grandson. I'll call Max to take you to the clinic."

"No need for that. I drove here all by my own damn self; I can definitely take myself to the clinic. No reason for anyone to be in a panic."

Martha just looked at her granddaughter a bit sternly. "It's his child too. He has a right to know."

Christine sighed. "Okay then fine. I'll go tell him," she said stomping grumpily out of the room calling Max' name.

"I'm here," he said appearing as if by magic in the hallway and startling Christine quite badly. More than was warranted she thought.

'Ugh do I have a B$_{12}$ deficiency or what?' she thought with self disgust.

"Uh hi," she said to Max.

"Hi," Max replied walking toward her. "Something wrong?"

"You could say that...er not really it's just precautionary you know," she said with a nervous laugh.

Max frowned. "Chris? Tell me what's wrong," he said in a tone that brooked no opposition.

Christine sighed wearily and then lifted her shirt again to show him the bruise. "I fell."

Max hurried forward, hand outstretched as if to touch the bruise… but he stopped just short of her skin, "Does it hurt?" he asked.

"Like a bitch," Christine said. "Gra thinks we should probably have it checked out just coz of the location and shit?"

"Oh. Yeah, she's probably right. Do you feel okay though?" he asked reaching out a hand to guide her gently into a seat like she might break if she stood for a moment longer.

"I'm fine. Really. Just you know, the pain…and the er, the baby. Worried," she mumbled.

"Andrea!" Max called and the clack of high heels on the uncarpeted corridor could be heard hurrying toward them from the study.

"Yes Max?" Andrea said coming to a halt at the door. Her eyes widened as she saw Christine…with Max' hand still on her shoulder with him bent solicitously toward her.

"I need you to call Dr. Mulholland and make an appointment for us as soon as possible. Now would be best."

"Er...us?" Andrea inquired in confusion. Clearly Max hadn't yet made the announcement to his staff that he was to be a father sooner rather than later. Christine lay back in the chair waiting to hear what he would say.

"Yes yes!" he replied irritably his impatience indicating that he wasn't as calm as he was trying to project. "Me and Christine."

"Er isn't your doctor's name Benson?" Andrea inquired.

Max turned to glare at her. "Andrea are you trying to get fired?" he ground out.

Andrea put up her hands in surrender. "Okay okay, I'll find this Dr. Mulholland's number and make the appointment," she said closing her mouth and regarding them for a moment as if waiting for further explanation. When none was forthcoming she opened her mouth again to make some inquiry but then changed her mind and closed it again.

"Okay then," she murmured with a shrug and went clacking down the corridor again.

"You should probably tell her," Christine said.

Max shrugged. "Not yet. Its too soon. Nobody needs to know yet but us."

Christine nodded her head in understanding. After all, people lost babies all the time. They might make some huge announcement and then not survive the first trimester. Case in point, her falling like a fool down a ladder. It was embarrassing but more than that, she was worried. Worried for her baby...she hadn't even been aware before this morning that she regarded it as *her baby*. Consciously, if she thought of it at all, she just imagined a bunch of ever multiplying cells holding her uterus hostage until they were ready to face the world. Now, all of a sudden, she was literally sick with worry that she might have inadvertently caused harm to her child. She'd read in the booklets that the amniotic fluid acted as a shock absorber to cushion the child from being hurt. She hoped to hell it was true in this case. But gra hadn't seemed worried so maybe she shouldn't worry either. Not that gra *would* tell her if she was worried. She had this whole 'keep calm in a crisis' policy that was easily misleading as to the seriousness of the situation if one paid attention to it.

"Could you get my grandmother please?" Christine asked Max.

"Yes of course," he replied straightening up and walking to the doorway. "Martha!" he called.

Christine smiled; it looked like Max was not ready to leave her alone even for the few minutes it'd take to get to the kitchen and back. A wave of cold washed over her as she remembered why he didn't want to do that. *What if the baby was hurt and she was just sitting here?* Maybe she should have gone to the hospital right away instead of seeking out her grandmother like she was wont to do in any situation.

"How are you and me going to be wed when my grandmother's your housekeeper? Don't you find that extremely super awkward?"

Max shrugged. "It's up to her what she wants to do. I was thinking you could both just move in and she could continue to run the house as sort of matriarch of the family or something," he said very absentmindedly, still keeping an eye on the door for Martha while gently running his hand up and down her back in a gesture she supposed he meant to be soothing. She wasn't sure if it was having the desired effect though. Oh it was doing *something* to her alright;

making soft parts softer and melting hard parts of her but she wasn't really paying attention to that now.

"You've really thought about it huh?" she said through a haze of what she didn't want to think of as lust.

"I've thought about it enough to know that we probably can't keep the status quo after the wedding. I also know your grandmother loves her house because I've offered repeatedly to move her into a suite of rooms here but she always refuses. Even though you would have gone to a much better run public school if you were in this neighborhood."

"Hey! There was absolutely nothing wrong with the school I went to," she protested.

"Oh yeah? Didn't you have a weapons check at the door?" he asked with a slightly superior raised eyebrow.

"Welcome to America bitch."

Max snorted and opened his mouth to reply when Martha walked in. "What seems to be the problem?" she asked.

"Nothing; Chris wants you," Max said sweeping his hand in her direction.

Christine grinned nervously at Martha. "Hey," she said with a small wave. Martha walked toward her and put her hand on her forehead, pulling her head forward to rest on Martha's stomach.

"Poor baby, you're scared out of your wits aren't you? Don't worry, everything will be alright," she said as she smoothed Christine's hair over and over. Christine buried her head in her grandmother's softness and exhaled.

*****

The doctor did an ultrasound so they could see that the little bundle of cells was currently busy exploring its environment and looking not at all moved that its host had had an accident but a few hours before.

"I mean of course you have to take better care and I would strongly advise if possible, that you avoid ladders and other risky activities especially for the next three months but otherwise, I think you're doing well. And the baby is doing well."

"Right. Thank you Dr. Mulholland," Christine said. She realized her hand was enveloped by Max' and they were clinging tightly to each other as the doctor gave the verdict. She couldn't hate though. This had been more nerve wracking than she'd imagined.

"My nerves are wracked," she said to him as they walked to reception to set up their next appointment.

"Mmmhmm," Max replied absentmindedly. Christine peered curiously at him, wondering at the sudden distance but didn't say anything because they were at reception and he was busy scheduling their next appointment.

"I'll call Stevens to come around to the entrance," she told him as she lifted her phone to her ear. It was a testament to how worried he'd been that he'd had Stevens drive them to the appointment. He usually enjoyed driving and usually only used Stevens for official company business. But today he'd sat in the back holding Christine's hand and making jokes about the poor kid having no chance to grow up as a girl's girl, what with her tomboy of a mom and a dad in the car business.

"Don't stereotype us," she'd protested making him laugh.

Maybe he'd sat in the back to calm *her* down and not because he was anxious....Christine didn't like to think about how much they were behaving like they were a couple or something. It was just... misleading and they should stop. If they were to have a marriage of convenience, there should be rules and regulations. He couldn't just run his hands down her back and make her feel things and then hold her hand as if he cared for her. That wasn't...what they agreed.

Christine walked toward the clinic doorway to wait for the car there. When she saw the black Bentley rounding the corner she walked toward it without waiting to see if Max was with her. They needed to stop the whole 'joined at the hip' vibe that she was beginning to get; before it became a problem. Stevens came around to open the door for her, studying her curiously as if he wanted to ask what all that was about but not sure about their boundaries. She hadn't interacted much with him in the past. He was just the driver who was usually downstairs in the garage with the cars; polishing them or maintaining them or whatever it was he did. They might exchange cordial nods if they ran into each other but that was it. She smiled tentatively at him, not wanting him to think...she didn't know what she didn't want him to think. Man, this pregnancy thing really seemed to be playing havoc with her emotional stability she thought.

Max came and slipped into the car, saying nothing about her leaving him at the reception by himself.

"Next appointment is next month on the ninth," he informed her.

She nodded her head, raising her phone to punch the information into her calendar as Max continued to study her.

"Are you okay?" he asked.

"I am great," she replied not knowing why she suddenly had a lump in her throat and a great desire to just...bawl into Max' shoulder.

"God, I hate pregnancy hormones," she said instead.

"Are you already feeling those?" Max asked curiously.

Christine shrugged. "It's a roller coaster in here baby," she said. Max laughed and slung an arm around her shoulders, rubbing gently at it in an absent minded manner. His thoughts seemed to be preoccupying him quite a bit.

"What are you thinking about?" she asked.

He widened his lips in what she supposed he took for a smile and looked her in the eye. "Well if you must know, I was wondering what would be the best way to ask you to move in with me?"

Christine stared at him, "Is that really necessary?"

"Maybe not *necessary* per se but it's something I would really appreciate if you could find it in your heart to do so."

"Why?" she asked leaning closer to him. Mostly because the massaging of her shoulders was making her melt into a puddle of content and she didn't feel like holding herself up but also so she didn't miss a single expression on his face.

"I want to take care of you," he said completely spoiling the mood. Christine sighed irritably and straightened up.

"I don't need you to-" she began.

"I know you don't need me. I know that," he cut in. "That's why I'm asking if you wouldn't mind too terribly if I did it anyway."

"And if I do mind?" she challenged, staring at him with unblinking eyes.

Max shrugged. "If its too much of a hardship for you, then there is very little I can do about it. I can't force you after all."

"That is true," she replied.

"But will you consider it?"

Christine turned her head to look at him properly. "I guess...well I guess you have every right to experience every moment of this pregnancy as much as I do. But just to be clear, staying in the same house doesn't mean that we...you know."

We...what?" Max asked in what *looked* like genuine puzzlement.

"We don't...you know...do it," Christine said her face hot.

Max stared at her in puzzlement for almost five minutes before his face cleared. "Oh you mean sex," he grinned.

"Yes, I mean sex. Don't think I don't know how you French men are."

"Hey! I'm only half French. And it's my American parent who's a slut."

"Well good on her. So now that we've cleared all that up," Christine said making a circle with her hand to encompass their conversation. "We can agree that yes, I'll be moving in but to my own room."

"Your own suite of rooms in case your grandmother can be enticed to join you."

"I wouldn't count on it but hey…I'm not saying no to that suite."

Max clapped his hands once. "Great, I'll get someone in to redecorate to your exact specifications."

Christine opened her mouth to protest the lack of necessity for that but Max was already shaking his head in rejection of her sentiments.

"That's what we're doing. I want you to be comfortable and feel at home. You won't do that surrounded by *my* things. You're not a guest – this is to be your home."

Christine lifted a hand to stop his diatribe,."I get it," she said with a wry twist of her mouth. Max' eyes dropped to her lips – she was wearing dark lipstick again today and when her lips were twisted like that it was like she was just inviting him to kiss…he dropped his eyes to get away from temptation but they landed in the v made by her jacket. Her shirt was also low slung so he could see the twins peeking out. If he wasn't mistaken, they were slightly bigger than before. Trust Christine to reap all the advantages of being pregnant; glowing skin, bigger breasts...without all the swollen ankles, bad breath and awkwardness. Or maybe that was still to come. This was his first time being so close to a pregnant lady; he didn't know.

"Are there classes we can take on what to expect?" he asked suddenly very anxious at his complete lack of knowledge.

"I think so. Probably. I can make inquiries," Christine offered.

"Don't tire yourself, I'll tell Andrea to do it."

"I thought you didn't want to tell anyone yet."

"Yes, but we need someone to assist us; at least we can trust Andrea not to go blabbing to the press."

Christine nodded. "Hey, you're the boss," she said with another twist of her mouth that evoked an answering twist at the level of Max' pelvis. For a moment, it was all he could do to keep breathing steadily.

"Yes," he said faintly. "I'm the boss."

Chapter 6

Christine called a family meeting the following Sunday; unlike Max she was close with her family and she needed them to know what was happening in her life. She didn't want to. The stain of what Rudy had done to her had not yet faded; her cousins still tended to look sympathetically at her when they were discussing their relationships. She had three that she was particularly close with; Sadie, Angela and Aisha. Their mother was her mother's cousin and she'd spent just as much time at their house as she had at her grandmother's growing up. Martha and her sister Misha were close since they were orphaned early in life and had no-one but each other for a long time. That closeness translated into their families growing up extremely intertwined. This closeness was exacerbated when they both lost their husbands to the war in Vietnam. They helped each other raise their kids; Martha had one girl; Cordelia and Misha had two boys; Andrew and Carl. Cordelia got pregnant in high school by a basketball player (she said) who disowned her and her baby before Christine was even born. Cordelia still named her after him. Andrew was the oldest of them all and pretty fertile by all accounts. He had three girls by three different women almost simultaneously, around the same time as Cordelia's pregnancy. He was doing relatively okay in his career and didn't want to pay child support so he applied for and obtained sole custody for all three babies. He then proceeded to leave them to his uncomplaining mother to raise. Still, he and his brother Carl chipped in and were very present in the lives of all four girls. It was an open secret that Carl was gay so nobody was expecting offspring from him anytime soon.

Martha provided food for the gathering but everyone chipped in with the making of it. Andrew and Carl were manning the grill outside making sure that the barbecue was coming along just fine. Cordelia and her man Kevin were mixing drinks while Martha took care of the hash browns and gravy. Christine was on corn on the cob duty while Sadie and Aisha took care of the pie. Angela was known to burn water so she was laying the table as she updated everyone on the neighborhood gossip.

"You know those new people who moved into number 22?" she asked as she gathered a pile of plates together. "The ones with the huge ass box of recording equipment? I heard they're independent porn producers."

Christine laughed, "You thinkin of applyin Ange?"

Angela threw a towel at her.

"Hey! No throwing my clean stuff around the kitchen," Martha growled.

"Sorry gra," Angela said sticking her tongue out at Christine behind Martha's back.

"Who told you that?" Sadie asked ignoring their playful fighting.

"Crazy Sandra. She heard it from Leroy over at the corner store."

"Oh yeah, very reliable," Christine said.

"So how would you explain it then?"Angie challenged, her hands crossed.

Christine shrugged. "I haven't thought about it. However, if I really feel like I'll die if I don't know I'll just cross over and ask them," she said causing Angela to kick her in the shins. Yes, the girls were close, and like all close siblings, they had their fights and arguments. Fights could flare up and flare out in the blink of an eye.

"Ouch. Careful now before you hurt someone," Christine said.

"Well if *someone* doesn't wanna get hurt they better can it with the crazy talk," Angie shot back.

Christine put up her hands. "Hands up, don't shoot."

Angie flipped her the bird but went back to her table arranging.

Once the food was done, they all sat down and Misha said Grace as they all linked hands. After the 'amens' were said they all dug in and the table was relatively quiet for a bit. Midway through the meal, Christine began to feel a little queasy but hoped it would pass. The barbecue had been made extra spicy in classic Uncle Andrew style and the combined smell of vinegar and garlic was assaulting her nostrils pretty bad. She tried taking shallow breaths to escape from the nausea but abruptly stood and ran as she lost the battle to keep her food down. She only just made it to the kitchen sink before she was projectile vomiting everything she'd eaten since the beginning of time. It was mortifying and Christine was glad that the only people who were there to see it were family...and Kevin. She didn't care about him so she wasn't worried what he did or did not see. In fact, she would really have been happy if her mother had just not come with him but she couldn't control that so she just shrugged inwardly and told herself that her mother would have told him anyway even if he hadn't been here.

"Hey are you okay?" Uncle Andrew was already rubbing soothingly against her back while Aisha handed her a towel to wipe her mouth and Angela washed out the sink. Christine took as long as she could wiping her face and nodding that she was fine before she looked up into her uncle's concerned eyes and smiled.

"I have something to tell you guys," she said as she leaned against the kitchen counter. Everyone who wasn't already watching her looked up from their plates now.

"Lemme guess; you're pregnant," Uncle Carl said totally stealing Christine's thunder.

"Uh..." Christine replied at lost for words for a moment. Uncle Andrew leaned forward so he could see her face properly. "You're pregnant?" he said sounding unflatteringly incredulous. "I didn't even know you were seeing anyone."

"Yeah neither did I," Angela said looking very aggrieved.

"Hey, you wanna sit down?" Sadie asked linking arms with her and leading her back to her seat. Christine was grateful for the temporary distraction. Sadie was really good at that shit; knowing exactly what people needed when they needed it.

Aisha placed a tall glass of water next to Christine and she drank carefully. Her mother was staring at her with wide eyes, as if she knew something and was just waiting for Christine to confirm it. Grandma Misha was watching her sister who was quietly eating her corn on the cob. Christine took a deep breath.

"I *am* pregnant," she confirmed leading to an eruption of conversation, everyone trying to talk over everyone else; asking questions, exclaiming and generally making it very difficult for Christine to explain anything.

"Everybody keep quiet," Martha snapped cutting the noise level off as if there was a mute switch she'd pressed somewhere. She gestured to Christine. "Continue," she said.

Christine took a deep breath and then breathed out, trying to calm her frantically beating heart. "It's gra's boss. Mr. Lestrange. He and I decided together that we wanted to have a child. Together. Since... well," Christine shrugged looking down at her plate. "You all know I ain't been seein anyone and Max thought he might have something that would render him unable pretty soon. So we thought, hey, why not save everyone a lot of grief and just do this thing together?"

"I don't understand," Uncle Carl was frowning as if he'd been presented with Einstein's equation and asked to break it down. "You and this Max guy decided to have a baby because he can't get it up?"

Christine breathed for five minutes, eyes closed and tried again. "Max was sick, right?" she said.

Various 'Uh huhs', were heard around the table.

"And the doctors told him that one of the side effects to his disease and its treatment might be that he can't have children," she continued looking around to see if this was sinking in. Some people were nodding, some were just staring at her.

"So anyway, Max has always wanted kids and so have I. Seeing as I'm not in a relationship and the ol' biological clock is ticking, when he came to me and...suggested that we have a baby, I agreed."

There was silence around the table.

"You done los' your damn mind," Angela was the first to break it.

"How pregnant are you?" Aisha asked. Always the practical one.

Christine shrugged, "About six weeks."

Misha turned to Martha, "You knew about this?"

Martha nodded her head but said nothing. Everyone stared at her in shock.

"And you let her do it?" Andrew asked what they were all thinking.

"It wasn't a matter of letting. They're both adults. It was their choice," she said.

Uncle Carl was glaring at Cordelia. "You awfully quiet sis," he said with a bit of a growl.

Cordelia looked up at him and shrugged. "Like mama said, she a big girl. If she want to have a baby with a billionaire I ain't hating on that child support," she said making Christine shrink in her seat. She was beginning to think this might have been a mistake. She wasn't here for her mother's grasping ways. Martha looked at her daughter with narrowed eyes.

"You really think your daughter would stoop to that level of thinking?" she snarled at her.

Cordelia shrank back in her seat, hands held open in supplication. "Hey, sorry. I was just telling it like I see it."

Martha stared thoughtfully at her. "Where did I go wrong with you?" she asked her.

Cordelia stared back at her and then back down at her plate. She shrugged her shoulders. "Just because I'm not interested in having a dry ass pussy like you and Aunt Misha or am not afraid of living like Christine here is, don't mean there's something wrong with me."

There was a collective intake of breath round the table. Martha's face was wooden and Misha looked like she was about to throw down. Uncle Andrew stood up walked around the table and lifted Cordelia from her seat with one hand. "Time for a time out," he said dragging her away toward the living room. "You can come back when you learn how to speak to people young lady," they heard him say as he led her kicking and screaming. Kevin sat stiffly looking around at them as if waiting for someone to jump on *him.*

"Perhaps you should go console your girl," Uncle Carl told him.

Kevin stood up at once and left. Pretty soon they heard the roar of his engine as they screeched out of the driveway. Uncle Andrew strolled back in minutes later looking like he'd just kicked ass and taken names.

"We good?" he asked the group at large.

There were various sounds of assent made around the table and Andrew took his seat looking at Christine.

"So...is this guy going to marry you or what?"

There was a collective wince around the table at the question. No one ever talked about marriage in Christine's hearing if they could help it.

Christine shrugged trying to look nonchalant. "He proposed."

Martha showed surprise for the first time that day, "What? When?"

"That time we went for coffee," Christine told her.

"Oh. He said..." Martha trailed off.

"He said what?" Christine asked sitting up with interest.

Martha shrugged, "he asked me what I thought of the idea of you two getting married."

"And you said?" Christine found she was holding her breath.

"I said...that it was a conversation he should have with you, not me."

"Well I guess he took your advice."

"And you said *yes*?" Martha was clearly surprised at this turn of events.

"I said that I would think about it," Christine qualified.

"Well what are you gonna say?" Angie wanted to know.

Christine shrugged. "I'll let you know as soon as I decide. For now, you need to know that I'm pregnant, I'm moving in with Max, strictly platonic," she said this last to her grandmother, "and we're gonna have a baby."

"Do you love him?" Sadie asked.

Christine laughed in surprise. "I um, I've known him for years ever since gra started working for him fifteen years ago. I can't say I don't love him. I think we're friends…sometimes. Sometimes I hate him; especially when he's right. Am I *in* love with him? Nope. That would be even more stupid than being in love with Rudy," that last bit came out more breathless than she'd planned. She hadn't said Rudy's name out loud since the wedding.

"Well stupid or not, sometimes these things happen," Angie said with a shrug.

"Well it hasn't happened," Christine countered.

"Yet", said Sadie.

*****

Christine was packing her clothes, really slowly, and thinking about what Sadie had said. She wondered if there was a chance of that happening. How stupid would she have to be to give her heart to Rudy and then to Max? If ever there was a player to beat all players, it was Max. The parade of models, actresses and socialites in his life was endless; it wasn't even funny. But then she relaxed, as far as she knew, Rudy still had full custody of her heart so there was really no way it was available for Max to ravage. Besides Max wasn't interested in that; if he had been he had his chance to suggest on that memorable morning when they'd...done it.

"What are you thinking about?" a deep voice asked from her doorway startling her.

"Sex," she said turning to look at him.

He lifted his eyebrows.

"What happens in marriages of convenience? Does the wife have sex with the gardener and the husband with his assistant or what?"

Max shuddered. "Ugh don't even say it. Me and Andrea? And we don't have a garden. Though I suppose we could move; the kids are going to need somewhere to play."

"So many places to go in that reply. What's wrong with Andrea? Kids? As in plural? I haven't even settled in, in the house you currently have; now we're moving? And to get back to the original issue...what?"

Max laughed. "I don't know, okay? We're just going to have to play it by ear. But I do think we should think about moving though... eventually. Please don't sleep with the gardener?"

It was Christine's turn to laugh, "Okay."

"Am I so repulsive then?" he asked.

"What?" Christine asked confused.

"I notice you didn't include the option of sleeping with each other," he said.

"Yeah but it's a marriage of *convenience*," Christine pointed out.

"And don't you think it'd be *convenient* to have sex with each other?" Max asked. "Only if we are both agreeable, of course."

"And are we?" Christine asked head tipped to the side in curiosity.

"Are we what?"

"Agreeable."

Max shrugged, "I don't know about you, but I am perfectly agreeable."

"I'm really high maintenance."

"Oh?"

"Yeah. If I'm having sex with someone, I kind of have this thing where I don't expect them to be having sex with anyone else."

"Wow. That is high maintenance."

"Yeah."

"But I think I can swing it."

"Yeah?"

"Yes. Why not? I don't want you to have sex with other people either. Do unto others and all that."

"Wow, I so was not expecting that."

"I like to surprise," Max said smugly.

"How about you surprise me further by packing the rest of my shit?"

"Okay," Max said stepping toward her closet.

"Whoa dude, enough with the agreeableness, it's freaking me out. I'm gonna need you to start an argument right now or I'm spraying you with holy water."

Max laughed again, "Sometimes, you...think you're funny."

"Ha, look who's laughing."

"Hey, how about I hire some movers to take care of all this shit and we go get some ice cream instead. You're pregnant right? That means you have cravings?"

"Not yet. But I never say no to ice cream."

"Great. I'll get Andrea to take care of this."

"Did you tell her already?" Christine asked as she hooked an arm around Max' and let him lead her to the car.

"Yeah. I did. She didn't seem too happy about it for some reason."

"Maybe she has a thing for you."

Max snorted, "*Everybody* has a thing for me."

"Oh yeah? Do you think *I* have a thing for you?"

"Obviously."

"Dude, you gotta get me some of that LSD you're on. It obviously gives you excellent hallucinations."

"You can't have any; you're pregnant."

"Oh yeah. Dang. I guess it'll have to wait."

"Yeah, meanwhile, do you wanna do ice cream cups or shall we just go stockpile tubs in the fridge."

"That last one."

"Which reminds me; lemme call Andrea," he said as he fished out his phone.

*****

Andrea was *pissed*. It was supposedly her day off; Sunday was her day off, unless Max had something big going on. Like that time he was hosting Mayweather for the weekend and he'd needed her to fulfill the myriad of requirements Mayweather had in order to feel comfortable. She'd scoured the city for the very specific bubble bath he needed before he could take a bath and he only used one brand of peanut butter on his bread; which he wanted to eat so...it had been exhausting. But Max was an appreciative boss and her bonus for that weekend had paid for her Birkin bag. But *this*...how could this be happening? Max was having a baby with Martha's grand-daughter. The sentence even sounded wrong in her head. This was not supposed to happen. They were supposed to be working late one night and he was supposed to offer her a drink. They were supposed to get drunk; happy drunk, not wrecked, and then she'd lean forward and kiss him because obviously he wouldn't touch her first in case it became a case of sexual harassment which she never would have filed...before. When they kissed he would put a shaking hand gently on her breast and his breath would catch and he would tell her he had been waiting forever for this. And she would have said that she'd been waiting for it too. And they would...have sex on the rug and on the table and then his bed and he would ask her to never leave him.

He was not supposed to get the housekeeper's grand daughter pregnant and move her into his house.

*****

MAX LESTRANGE SPOTTED SHOPPING WTH MYSTERY WOMAN

Andrea saw the headline and clicked on the story wondering what the hell Max thought he was doing. There wasn't much of a story; just a picture of Max and Martha's granddaughter looking down at the ice cream fridge in the supermarket. They looked pretty cozy together; heads bent close to each other, pointing out flavors to each other...

'That should be me.'

The thought flashed through Andrea's brain faster than a bullet and her face closed in frustration.

'Why did he choose her*?'*

Andrea had a degree in Marketing and communications from Berkeley University. She wasn't just some dumb blonde. If it was brains Max was looking for she had those. She had beauty, poise, grace; she was the perfect life partner for a man like him. Why had he chosen this girl instead. Granted she was bright; she'd gotten into MIT with a full ride but that was about it. Her hair was a hot mess, she walked around in coveralls three quarters of the time and she was *black* for crying out loud. Wrong wrong wrong. Andrea straightened suddenly, a thought occurred to her.

'I bet your mother doesn't know about this.'

She thought at the picture of Max. How to have her find out without the trail leading back to Andrea was the challenge. If Max' mother knew what was happening, she'd take steps to stop it. She'd never let Max end up with someone so...unsuitable. And she might help Andrea out in her gratitude to get Max to notice her at last. It was worth a try.

*****

"It's them again," Cordelia told Kevin as she brought his beer from the fridge. She showed him her iPad which was opened on some tabloid that showed Christine and Max shopping together at the supermarket.

"They're calling her the 'mystery women'. You think they'd pay good money to know who she is?" Cordelia asked looking speculatively at the picture and then at Kevin. They were running low on funds since neither of them had a steady job. They mostly relied on government relief.

"I hear those niggas pay like millions for this kind of shit," Kevin said.

"How would we get to them to sell our story? Do we need to get lawyered up? We got the inside scoop after all."

"Yeah but…" Kevin hesitated. "What if your daughter like…disses us after that. We could go to this cat she with and tell him to pay us not to sell our story right? That way we ain't got to go to no tabloid and we still get money."

Cordelia regarded him with shining eyes, "You the bomb Kevin, you know that?"

Kevin nodded his head and smirked, "We still gotta get lawyered up doh; you know this guy's got like lawyers on lawyers on lawyers on retainer. We gotta protect our rights."

"Yeah," Cordelia nodded her agreement. "Pass the blunt."

*****

"So these are your rooms. We have a little sitting room for you to relax in, your bedroom and ensuite bath. There's a walk in closet and a small balcony," Max showed her around her new digs, pointing out all the amenities.

"It's sweet," Christine said impressed in spite of herself, "Where the baby room though?"

"I'm thinking we can put the nursery next door. I'm just opposite you so it'd be convenient for both of us."

"Mm," Christine said. "Works for me. Only can I have a crib in here in case like, I need to be close?"

Max smiled, "Whatever works for you."

"Cool."

They could hear the movers bumping about, trying to get things up the narrow stairs. There was a service lift but it stopped on the floor below. Luckily there wasn't much that was very bulky. Just a shelf of books that had been with Christine for as long as she could remember, her grandfather's phonograph that her grandmother had passed on to her since she loved music, and her collection of African masks. She didn't think Max had seen those yet so she still had something to surprise him with. She thought she could hang them all over the house like she had at home with her grandmother. If Max really meant it about this also being her home, he wouldn't object.

He turned to smile at her, "Welcome home Chris."

"Thank you," she replied with a smile. "Don't call me that."

Chapter 7

"Ladies and gentlemen, we're gathered here today to celebrate the joining of these two people in holy matrimony. If anyone has any objection to this union let them speak now or forever old their peace," the celebrant said.

Christine tensed, waiting for that inevitable objection. She felt her heart speed up and her breath come short. Anxiety was building in her chest and the preacher seemed to be taking a really long time to move on even if no-one was coming forward...this time. A hand covered hers and she looked down. It was a nice hand, the nails professionally cut short. Long lean fingers; but strong. A single blood vessel ran visibly from wrist to fingers. Christine liked that hand. She looked up from the hand to the face. It was Max. He was smiling at her.

"Are you alright?" he asked.

"I'm fine," she whispered. Her throat felt raspy.

His hand squeezed hers, "I'll take care of you."

Christine nodded. She realized she wasn't the one at the altar; this wasn't her aborted wedding. She looked forward to see whose wedding it was but the altar was empty. No priest, no bride, no groom. Christine's brow furrowed with puzzlement.

"What's happening?" she asked Max.

"This is *your* dream. You tell me," he said.

"Maybe I don't need it anymore," she said. "Maybe it's changing."

"Maybe you want it to change," he said.

Christine woke up with a cry, breath coming fast, to an unfamiliar room. She looked around her, wondering where she was for a moment before she remembered. She was in Max' house, in her new suite of rooms. She looked at the opposite wall to see her wood African mask looking back at her. A knock on the door startled her.

"Chris? You okay?" Max called from the other side.

"I'm fine thanks," she called back.

"Can I come in?" he said.

Christine leaned back on her headboard. She really did not want to be alone right now. "Sure, come in."

Max opened the door tentatively. He was dressed in a black track suit bottom and nothing else. Christine stared at him unable to take her eyes off his chest. His muscles rippled in toned ruggedness. One wouldn't know it from his appearance while clothed...and it had been a while since Christine had seen him without a shirt.

"Whoa," she murmured.

Max smiled. "You likey?" he asked without even a smidgeon of smugness; the only thing that saved him from permanent banishment from her presence.

Christine shrugged. "You have a mirror," she said matter of factly.

Max came to sit on the side of her bed still smiling, "So, what's up?"

"Nothing," Christine replied.

"I heard you cry out," Max protested.

"I had a bad dream. It happens."

Max stood up. "I'll get you a glass of hot milk then. I hear its good for what ails you."

"You don't have t-"

"I want to. It's what your grandmother would do, no?"

Seeing as it was indeed what her grandmother would do, Christine couldn't exactly protest. She lay back and waited for her hot milk, rubbing her stomach gently.

"Hey there," she whispered to it. "How you doing? You okay? Sorry about your stupid mama's stupid nightmares. I promise I'll try not to have them again."

The baby said nothing but Christine felt soothed anyway.

Max came back not long after with a mug of hot chocolate and a piece of chocolate fudge cake. Christine's eyebrow went up.

"Seriously?" she asked.

Max shrugged. "We're pregnant which means we're allowed," he peered at her. "You *do* want some don't you?"

"Only if you'll share with me," she said suppressing a smile.

Max sighed theatrically. "Only because you're carrying my baby."

Christine smirked, "You're too kind."

They sat in silence, eating and drinking in contentment. Max wriggled onto the bed so he was next to Christine leaning on the head board.

"Mmm," he said biting into the chocolate confection.

"Good?" Christine asked.

"Orgasmic," Max replied. Christine found that her cheeks were hot even as she laughed. She reached out with a finger to scrape some chocolate cream off the top of the cake and sucked her finger into her mouth. Max watched the progress of her finger, staring as she sucked the succulent cream off her hand. His eye caught hers and held it and then swooped down to look at her finger. His mouth opened slightly and his tongue peeked out as his eyes followed the movement of her hand. He leaned forward slightly seemingly without meaning to and Christine plopped the finger out of her mouth.

"What?" she asked in a tiny voice.

Max said nothing, just continued to stare at her mouth as she watched him. His tongue came out and ran itself along his lips.

"Dry lips? You want some hot chocolate?" she asked in that small voice.

"Sure," he said and his voice was just as low. He reached out to take it from her hand and took a sip, his eyes not leaving hers.

"Mmmm," he said.

"Good?" she asked, her mouth unconsciously pouting.

"Very," he said and then suddenly he was kissing her. It happened so fast Christine didn't have any time to have thoughts about it. His mouth was surprising soft and gentle, his lips touched hers. But underneath the softness there was demand for entry, and urgency. Christine couldn't help but respond to it, softening her own lips, leaning forward and parting her lips to allow his entry. That seemed to be the signal he was waiting for because his arms closed around her like an iron vice and he held her close against his chiseled chest. Christine's arms went about his neck and she arched into him inserting her tongue as deep into his mouth as his was in hers. Max' hands began to wander, pulling up her spaghetti top. He detached his lips from hers for a moment so he could sling the shirt off her head and fling it to the far corner of the room with a flick of his finger. Then his mouth was back, biting gently into her bottom lip as he made the same sounds he'd been making when he was eating the cake. His mouth left her lips, tongue trailing along her skin before he sucked gently on her chin.

"Are you eating me?" she croaked.

"You're delicious," he said pulling her closer and tipping her over on the bed. Christine straightened out her legs under him and his hands immediately landed on either side of her hips and began worrying at her silken shorts. She helped out by wriggling so he could pull them out from under her and toss them in a different corner from the shirt. His pelvis ground against her naked belly and she could feel just how 'happy' he was to see her. She reached between them and dug into his track suit, grasping firmly at his dick and pulled. He let out a surprised gasp and then jerked forward as if encouraging her to do it again. She pulled again harder and he uttered a small protest.

"Careful; it's no good to you if you pull it off," he murmured licking against her neck.

Christine giggled, changing her grip from a pull to a massage. Not that he needed any more stimulation; it was like holding a bar of iron encased in a silk glove. Max' hands traveled downward clutching at the waist of his track suit and pulling it down to his thighs. He grasped her hips and widened them, thrusting forward so she could feel him along the length of her entrance.

"May I?" he groaned as he continued to grind against her inner thigh, his powerful body held in check, but only just.

Christine's hands trailed downward and settled on his ass, pulling him forward, saying better than words that he may. He breached her with one unbridled thrust as he gasped aloud and she cried out. His thrusting thereafter was demanding and uninhibited in its urgency and he threw his head back and let it rip as she wrapped her legs around him and held on.

"Oh God, so good," she murmured as he pounded into her.

"Am I hurting you?" he ground out, breath harsh and loud in the still midnight air.

"Harder," she replied into his ear.

He made a sound like he hurt a lot and redoubled his efforts.

Christine could feel the tension building inside her and she knew that release was near. Her eyes closed of their own volition and her back arched in readiness for ecstasy. Suddenly, Max pulled out of her but before she could utter a cry of protest he'd flipped her over so her ass was in the air. She was so startled she hardly noticed when he slammed into her again almost making her face plant into the side of the bed. She held grimly onto the sheet as he proceeded to pound her into the mattress. Christine widened the angle of her thighs so he could have better access, hoping in a vague sort of way that this was not hurting the baby. Then she remembered the amniotic fluid and calmed down, or as much as she could with Max creating all sorts of sensations inside her body. Hot sensations, cool sensations, electrical pulse sort of sensations...ballooning feelings of impeding nuclear explosion centered at her center. It really was not fair that he could do this to her. The only thing that consoled her was that judging from the tomato hue of his skin, the bulging veins around his eyes, his wide eyed staring and deep ass loud breathing... he was feeling it too.

"Max?" she whispered in moaning desperation.

"Yes," he replied going faster and deeper as he did so and making her completely lose her train of thought. She leaned forward, placing her weight on her elbows and widening access to her inner self. Max wasn't slow to respond, burrowing even deeper into her so that she felt like she might be feeling him in her throat pretty soon.

"So good...love this...*God*," he was murmuring behind her, or he could just be saying random words. Christine put her head down and let go, her whole body loosening and softening. Then Max arched his back and let out a pained groan and before she knew what was coming she felt his wetness spreading inside of her as his body jerked uncontrollably. She suppressed a sigh of disappointment; so close yet so far.

The strong salt-musky taste of Christine made Max' head swim and his heart flutter frantically in his chest. Christine not only looked irresistible lying there so needy and desperate; she was fucking gorgeous. Christine felt like she was drowning, held down by the weight of her own desire. She was helpless to do anything other than keep Max caught inside her, straining like a butterfly half-smothered by honey. He withdrew himself slowly, much to her disappointment but his penis was replaced soon after by finger and tongue and soon Christine was, honest to God, sobbing as her body broke apart and fell like rain on to the pristine cream covers they were lying on. For a while, everything went white.

"Chris? Baby? Are you okay?" she heard Max ask after an interminable time went by.

"Don't call me that," she mumbled into the pillows.

"Okay," he said, his voice torn between uncertainty and amusement. "I'll get you some water shall I?"

Christine made an incoherent sound that could be consent and she felt the bed dip as Max got off. She closed her eyes, completely unable to keep them open or her brain active for another second. All her circuits were fried. She felt like she was in deep trouble here.

*****

Max staggered to the kitchen; he felt kind of dizzy, kind of drunk, kind of high. At the back of his head though, a voice kept chanting, 'whatdidyoudowhatdidyoudowhatdidyoudo?' like some sort of hoodoo mantra that would somehow make everything clear. He was through the looking glass here with no road map on how to proceed. He got the water from the dispenser and took the glass carefully back to Christine. She was passed out on the bed and didn't respond to his calls so he put the glass down gently on the bedside table and pulled the duvet out from under her, and covered her with it. She didn't so much as stir. He watched her sleep for a moment, unable to move away or move forward. Should he stay with her? What would she think if she woke in the morning beside him? What would she think if she woke up and he wasn't beside her? What to do for the best?

Despite all her bravado, Max knew she still hurt for that bastard Rudy's rejection; she was still a fragile petal – easily broken. He had no intention of breaking her…so maybe having sex with her like that had been an extremely bad idea. Max gave a shrug; it was way too late to unspill that milk so all there remained to do was find a way forward; out of this quagmire. Or maybe it didn't have to be a quagmire? Maybe it was just a natural progression of their relationship. They were to be married after all…that's what it came down to. He needed to get that prenup signed so she couldn't back out. If he'd succeeded in spooking her; she *would* back out. She couldn't though; she already carried his child. And they had agreed even without signing anything. She was a woman of her word; she would not back out now....would she?

Max walked out of the room, his head spinning. He crossed to his room and picked up the phone from his dresser, dialing without thinking.

"This better be life and death young man. It's two o' clock in the mornin," Martha growled.

"I just had sex with Chris," Max replied without preamble. "What should I do now?"

Martha was silent on the other end. "I don't believe this is my area of expertise," she said slowly.

"You know her, you know me; do you think she's gonna run in the morning?"

"Where is she now?"

"Passed out on her bed."

"Okay then. I suggest you get some rest and have a rational

discussion with her come daylight. And the next time y'all indulge in whatever behavior, *do not call me in the middle of the night,"* Martha said before hanging up.

Max stared at the phone and then dropped it on the bed. Well that hadn't been as helpful as he'd hoped. He gave himself that shrug again and decided to take her advice anyway; he'd sleep on it and see what happened in the morning.

*****

The puking woke him up in the morning. For a moment he wondered if he'd picked up some random drunk model who was now puking her hangover into his facilities but then he'd remembered exactly why his dick felt misused and sat up quickly. His door was open, and so was hers and that's why he could hear the sounds of last night's dinner hitting the toilet bowl from here. His rooms tended to be quite sound proof otherwise. He ventured out of bed and padded over to her room, knocking tentatively at the door before letting himself in and crossing over to the open bathroom door. Christine's dark head was so far down the toilet bowl it had almost disappeared and her whole body was heaving.

Max wanted to ask her if he could be of assistance but he was afraid she was puking because of what they did last night. If that was so, he didn't want to be a reminder that would make her throw up more.

Eventually, her head came up out of the bowl and she crouched back, breathing hard as she tried to get her bearings. He walked silently to the sink, wet a towel and brought it quietly to her. She took it and wiped off her mouth and then handed it back to him.

"You alright?" he asked tentatively.

"I'm peachy," she said standing up and crossing to the sink to wash her face and rinse out her mouth.

"Is there anything I can do for you?" he asked again.

"No. Well, yes. Get me a glass of orange juice if you can," she said and he hurried off to the kitchen to do as he was told. Christine drank it down and then asked if there was any bacon for breakfast, with some sausages, some eggs, hash browns, and one muffin...or two.

Max took that for the order it was and went to see what the cook could rustle up. Unlike Martha, he lived in, in the 'service wing' upstairs so he was on call at all hours. He got right on that as Max went back to report that her breakfast was on hand.

"Thanks, now would you excuse me? I'd like to change."

"Yes of course," Max replied and went to his own room to have his own shower. he was hoping that by the time he came out, Martha would have arrived to tell him what to do next.

Chapter 8

Pregnancy was hard; no in fact it was impossible. The mood swings, the constant pendulum between hunger and nausea, the heightened emotion; it was making Christine feel like a crazy person. If she wasn't careful she was going to end up killing somebody one of these days. Today was one of those days that she really needed everybody to stay away from her. she'd arrived at work to find her co-workers huddled in a conspiratorial group; clearly gossiping about something. It didn't take long for her to find out what the gossip was about. Leandra came by fishing for the tea, asking her about her love life and who she was seeing these days. Christine just glared at her. Just because they were the only two female engineers in their department didn't give Leandra the green light to know everything about her. It was still none of her damned business.

"Don't you have work to do?" she snarled. Her stomach was burning like she had hyper-acidity or something. She really was not in the mood to be diplomatic with anyone.

"Okay girl, be like that. I'm just sayin though, if you wanna have a secret romance don't do it with a famous dude and then let the paparazzi take photos of you," she said.

"What. The fuck. Are you talkin' bout Lele?" she asked or rather demanded.

Leandra hurried over to snatch the paper (Christine could see that is was a local tabloid) out of the hands of two interns and brought it eagerly over to her. She folded it solicitously so that Christine could clearly see the picture of her and Max at the supermarket looking over ice cream choices.

"Y'all look so cute together. I didn't know you were into the white meat. How come you refused to go out with my cousin Carlos when I set y'all up last year?"

Christine looked up to glare at Leandra, wondering what was the best way to tell her to fuck off.

"It's really none of your business you know," she said handing the paper back to her. "Who said I'm even dating that guy?"

"Y'all looking all terribly familiar and all. What? You gon' say he's just a friend?" Leandra was smirking. Christine was not in the mood to tolerate smirking.

"Think whatever the fuck you like. I got work to do," she said shoving rudely past the other girl as she headed to her locker to get her uniform out. She knew that she hadn't heard the last of it but she just did not have the time right now. Her stomach was beginning to feel queasy again. She was afraid for a moment that she would upchuck her breakfast right there in the locker room, in front of her subordinates. She grabbed her uniform quickly and hurried off to the ladies wanting to get out of sight just in case her body betrayed her. Just as she closed the door of the stall behind her and began to undress, she was startled badly by her phone ringing. The ringtone was 'beautiful loser' by Bob Seger so she knew it was Max on the other end.

"Did we decide what we were going to tell people?" she asked without preamble.

"Er, no. But tell them whatever you want," he said, French accent coming through loud and clear. It thickened when he was under stress.

"What's wrong?" she asked.

"We need to talk. Soon," he said.

"What's happened?"

"Not on the phone. I'll pick you up at lunch time."

"I don't know where I'll be at lunchtime."

"That's why you have a phone, and I have a phone and we can call each other and find out."

"Don't be rude."

"Don't be difficult."

"I'm pregnant, I'm allowed to be difficult."

"I'm sorry, you're right; you're pregnant and crazy which translates to difficult. I'll try to deal."

"You're talking yourself out of that lunch date bro," she warned.

"Trust me, you don't want to stand me up," he said and hung up. Christine sighed. She could spend the whole morning worrying and giving herself more heartburn or she could eat chocolate and pretend that everything was awesome. She chose option two just cause it involved chocolate and she had some in her pocket. Also, she didn't really have much fondness for worrying – too many years of her life had been wasted on that. Now she just wanted to get through this pregnancy without becoming 5150 and that would mean making healthy choices. Like chocolate.

It wasn't helpful that they hadn't discussed the incredible sex they'd had the night before. Granted, Christine was up early and puking her guts out which Max might have taken askance. Perhaps he thought she was disgusted by his behavior last night? She didn't know how she felt about it, but it definitely wasn't disgust. Or maybe *he* was disgusted...Maybe he needed to give her The Talk; the one where he reminded her that this was a marriage of convenience and she shouldn't read too much into last night. Like she would. Obviously it was a booty call; inadvertent maybe but by now she knew how those worked. The guy appeared in your room in the middle of the night and he was gone by morning. Just like what had happened last night. She wasn't dumb, maybe she was slow but she'd gotten it eventually with Rudy. She didn't need a second lesson.

Christine finished changing and got on with her shift. She was on half day today because next week she'd be on night duty. She wondered if she should inform HR that she was pregnant...she wasn't familiar with what the protocol was but she didn't want to involve herself in situations that were dangerous to her child. Christine resolved to look those up as well because she wasn't sure what was dangerous and what wasn't.

"Hey Chris," Fred Jones murmured to her as they passed each other on the stairs. "How's tricks?"

Christine looked into his face to see if there was more to the greeting than just...greeting but couldn't read much in his impassive face.

"Good, good. You?" she asks in return.

Fred shrugged, "Night shift man."

Christine nodded because she knew how those could be sometimes; they could go from excruciatingly boring to reluctantly exciting. Christine was strongly in favor of the former. She walked on to her work station and got to work, dismissing all the things swirling in her head; for now.

*****

Max took her to a semi-fancy restaurant and explained to her that it has the widest menu of any place he's been to in the city. So whatever she felt like eating, they'd probably find it. Christine was grateful because she'd been thinking about chicken nuggets all morning but also fried fish. She studied the menu and saw that they have both these items much to her delight, plus some baked potatoes, baby carrots and salad. She figured that would do...to start with.

"God, I'm going to weigh a ton by the time this kid is born," she wailed.

"No you won't because you're on your feet all day and you'll work it all off," Max consoled, patting her hand.

"Yeah okay, we'll go with that version," Christine agreed. "Now I want to enjoy my food so how about you tell me why you brought me here so I can know?"

Max took a deep breath looking solemn. "I received a call from a lawyer this morning," he said watching her.

"And?" she asked sipping on the water that had been placed on the table.

"And…he represents a couple of clients who know about our deal and are threatening to take it to the press unless we pay them off," he finished.

Christine froze, looking up at him. "Who are these people?"

"He wouldn't say. But he did give me enough detail for me to know that they are for real. They know about our deal."

"Who do you think it is?" Christine asked, her heart speeding up. She has a very bad feeling about this.

Max shrugged. "I have no clue but I can get investigators on it."

Christine thought hard. "Give me a day or two first before you do that. I might be able to get to the bottom of this without it getting messy."

"Okay, if you think that's best," Max said.

Christine was surprised at his unprotesting capitulation but since it's what she wanted, she was not about to argue.

"Okay then," she said with a nod.

The waiter brought the first course and she dug in.

*****

The tabloids were full of stories and conjecture about the mystery girl Max Lestrange was dating. She doesn't remain a 'mystery girl' for long. Somebody spilled; her name, where she works…not much else so Christine guessed it's probably Leandra or someone else from the office. She was pissed about it but there was very little she could do. She was more taken aback at all the fake stories that now abound about her 'relationship' with Max. Everything from her age to her ethnicity was altered to fulfill whatever fantasies the tabloid wished to conjure up this week. In one story she was a stripper who Max met and was smitten with and she's now his official mistress as if they're living in eighteenth century England, in another she blackmailed him into being with her because she knew secrets about his past that he doesn't wish to come out; in some she's desperate to marry him for his money and is twisting his arm by trying to get pregnant – that one was uncomfortably close to the truth for comfort – so as to force him into matrimony. Christine felt like leaving town.

"Maybe we should put out a statement and explain what's really going on," she suggested to Max that night as they have dinner. Martha was still working as housekeeper because she refused to quit just because Christine is uncomfortable with the situation. She told her to deal with it; after all she's been Max' housekeeper for fifteen years without Christine finding it to be a problem. Max told her he's giving her notice that she's to move to head of housekeeping at Lestrange Enterprises by month's end and she was annoyed until he mentioned that the salary is three times what she's making. She decided she could probably live with that as long as Max wasn't doing it just because he's about to marry her granddaughter. He is...but he isn't. He wanted to keep Martha close but he knew she couldn't be his housekeeper. Not when she'd be obliged to take orders from her granddaughter. It just would not do. And she refused to stop working and just retire in splendor as matriarch of their new family so what was a man to do?

* * * * *

As soon as Christine was through with work, she dodged Leandra's persistent invitations to go 'have coffee', as well as Mary Jane's wanting to corner her to tell her all about the latest going on in her life with her mentally abusive yet apparently irresistible boyfriend. They broke up and made up almost on a weekly basis and Mary

Jane seemed to think Christine wanted to know all about it. In truth, she couldn't care less so when she saw MJ headed toward her she fished out her phone and called her cousin Sadie.

"Houston, we have a problem," she said into the receiver.

"What is the mayday about?" Sadie wanted to know.

"Somebody be snitchin," she said.

"About?" Sadie asked.

"About me and my situation."

"Who they snitchin to?"

"Paps," Christine said. "You need to call a meeting and find out who it was."

"How do you know it's not me?" Sadie asked.

"Is it?" Christine asked.

"Nope."

"Good, so you'll call the meeting?"

"Just us girls or everyone?"

"Everyone who knows."

"Okay for when?"

"It's urgent. If you can gather them tonight all the better. I'm headed to grandma's."

"I'll get back to you."

"Thanks Sadie."

"Uh huh."

*****

Sadie was as good as her word and she had everyone save Martha and Misha gathered in Martha's living room by 8:30pm that night. She'd even managed to get Kevin and Cordelia to attend on the pretext that there was some money to be discussed; she was vague about it but she might have implied that Max was giving out checks to enable them to shop for the wedding. She'd thought about padding the lie with implications of a private jet to New York for the shopping spree but the prospect of money alone was enough to get

Cordelia there so she figured that would do.

As soon as everyone gathered Christine stood up.

"Ladies and Gentlemen, we have a problem," she said looking at every face. Uncle Andrew lifted a brow at her. He had been expecting to be fed but Martha wasn't even home yet.

"What problem?" Uncle Carl asked.

"Somebody is trying to extort money out of Max otherwise they go to the press and tell them about us. Now the thing is not many people know about our deal, and the majority of them are in this room," Christine said looking around the room and bracing herself for outrage.

"And you think maybe somebody in this room is the culprit?" Uncle Carl asked his eyes on Cordelia.

"I think it's a distinct possibility, yes," Christine said also looking toward Cordelia with narrowed eyes.

"Who would want to do that?" Cordelia asked. "Are you saying one of your cousins is maybe jealous of you?"

Christine looked toward Sadie, Angela and Aisha, grouped together on the sofa. They looked back at her as if in challenge. She shook her head.

"I don't think it was them," she said and Angela beamed at her while Aisha and Sadie merely nodded.

"Then who?" Kevin demanded in an aggressive tone.

Christine said nothing for a while.

"Nothing irrevocable has happened yet. There is still time to change your minds."

She caught and held each and every one's eye trying to see who would flinch. Nobody did, but then her mother's glance slid away from her after a second of eye contact. She made as if to pick a non-existent piece of lint from her skirt and wouldn't look at Christine again. Christine sighed in tired resignation. It was always *something* with her mother; she really wished sometimes that she could just cut Cordelia loose and forget she ever existed. But then Cordelia was still her mother and try as Christine might she still loved her and still wanted her mother to be part of her life. It was stupid and it was probably going to get her in deep shit one day; in fact that day might be here right now but...blood was blood.

"Mother? Do you have anything you'd like to say to me?" she asked trying to still the tremble in her voice. Cordelia shook her head but didn't look up.

"Sis," Uncle Andrew hissed.

"I haven't done anything! Why y'all always pickin on me?" Cordelia shouted.

"Nobody's pickin on you C. We just asked you a question and you jumpin down peoples' throats and shit..."

Cordelia stood up. "I'm leavin," she said, she bent over and pulled at Kevin. "Come on Kevin, lets go."

Everyone watched them rush out like their hair was on fire and their tails were catching. Christine felt a knot in her chest, like a heaviness. It was there on and off every time she interacted with her mother. She always had hopes that never came to fruition. And now her mother had sicced lawyers onto her...er, she had no idea what to call Max; partner in crime? Fake husband? Marriage of convenience mate? Baby Daddy? She thought that last one might be the most accurate description.

"What now?" Sadie asked startling Christine out of her reverie.

Christine shrugged. "I have no idea. Uncle Andrew could you talk to her maybe? Make her see the error of her ways?"

"I've *been* talking to her. I love your mama like a sister but she is the messiest bitch I've ever known and she's not going to change now. It was a mistake to tell her anything."

"Yeah thanks for that input; not really helping with the situation," Christine said miserably.

There was a strained silence for a few minutes.

"Pre-emptive strike," Sadie said.

"What?" Christine replied.

"Release a statement to the public, telling them what's really happening," Sadie said.

Uncle Andrew was already shaking his head.

"Absolutely not; that would just open a whole new can of worms,"

Christine said. Uncle Andrew nodded his head in agreement.

"So what then?" Sadie asked.

"Pay them off, one time only and make them sign an NDA."

"Do you think they'll stick to it?"

"We'll emphasis to them that the penalty for talking would be compensation of twice the money they're paid. Since I absolutely guarantee they won't have it; they'll have to keep their traps shut."

"Unless they're offered substantially more than twice what you pay them," Aisha pointed out.

"Yeah, well that doesn't stop them from experiencing jail time."

"You would have her arrested? For real?" Angela asked.

"Yep," Christine said though she wasn't as confident as she tried to seem. Her mother was so complex. "God this sucks," she exclaimed.

Uncle Carl came over to her and enveloped her in his arms.

"Don't worry baby. It'll be alright," he said soothingly rubbing her back.

Just then her phone beeped. It was a text from Max.

Are you coming home?

She had clicked on the reply option before it occurred to her to wonder why he would care.

Not tonight.

She hit send and then turned back to her uncle and leaned into him.

"I'm gonna have to tell him. I'm gonna have to tell Max," she said almost hyperventilating.

"Shhh," Uncle Carl said.

The phone beeped again. Max again.

Why?

Christine frowned wondering at all this sudden interest.

I'm taking care of business.

She replied barely restraining herself from being rude. She stared at her phone waiting to see if he would reply and what he would say.

She was startled when the phone rang. Beautiful loser permeated the room before Christine pressed answer.

"What?" she said into the receiver as her family watched her.

"Where are you?" he asked.

Christine opened her mouth to tell him how he wasn't the boss of her when she remembered her audience. She put up a hand and murmured 'excuse me' before disappearing into the dining room.

"You're not the boss of me Max," she whispered into the phone.

"I'm concerned for you that's all. Can I come pick you up? It's late and you need your rest."

"I know what I need Max; and I'll thank you to back off."

"All your stuff is here. You're moved in. This is your home. This is where you sleep. So where are you?"

Christine sighed in irritation. "I'm at gra's house okay? Getting to the bottom of this snitch situation. Happy?"

It was Max' turn to sigh, "How about I come over, and help you out?"

"Thanks but I can manage."

Max began to say something else but Christine wasn't listening. "Listen," she said over his voice, "I'm gonna sort this shit out and then imma spend the night here. I'll see you tomorrow." She could practically feel him wanting to protest but all he said was;

"Okay then."

Chapter 9

Max was pacing. He didn't want to be; it was late and he was tired and he needed his rest. Especially after last night. But here he was unable to rest, unable to sleep; pacing. It was annoying as hell because a few months ago, he was a free agent with nothing on his mind except gambling and sex; he'd had his money on Mayweather in that bout and he and Kendal were going to 'take their relationship to the next level'. He wasn't too bummed that the latter hadn't happened but he had yet to collect his winnings from the former.

His life had been so much simpler then; he was coasting – escaping from the necessity to really grow up. Now he was confronted with his mortality, and was attempting to bring new life into the world. A wave of dizziness hit him at the thought and he staggered, aiming for the bed to avoid a face plant on the floor. He expected the dizziness to dissipate as he sat down, maybe a result of all the back and forth pacing but instead his vision blurred and he felt like the world was getting black around the edges. He had just enough presence of mind to hit the call button before he blacked out.

*****

When he came to, he found that he was in a moving vehicle going at speed. There was a mask over his face but as he tried to move his hand to remove it, he found that he could not. His hand was attached to several tubes that impeded his movement. He opened his eyes slowly to see a young blonde man with a buzz cut and vivid green eyes staring intently at him.

"Mr. Lestrange, are you alright?" he asked.

Max nodded his head trying to indicate with his eyes that he wanted the mask off his face. The man ignored him, listening to his heart beat with a stethoscope. Max recognized the uniform as belonging to his emergency rescue service but he hadn't met this particular EMT before. Of course it wasn't like he was a geriatric used to taking regular emergency trips to the hospital.

"Mr. Lestrange you seem to have a flare up of inflammation around your prostate judging by your elevated temperature and the slight shake in your extremities. Are you in pain? Just nod for yes or shake for no."

Max was about to shake his head when he felt it; a burning just above his pelvis. He nodded his head and tried to turn his eyes down toward the correct spot but the EMT was not paying attention. He was injecting something into the IV that was stuck in Max' arm. Max wanted to ask if someone had notified Christine; surprised at how much he wanted her by his side at this time. But then he remembered that Martha had been in the house when he passed out. She would inform her granddaughter and then Christine would come to him.

*****

Martha did try to call Christine but she was dead to the world and didn't hear the phone ring. She shrugged to herself, leaving a voicemail and then calling Whitby and Constantine to notify them that she'd had to call an ambulance to the house which probably meant someone would get hold of the news by tomorrow. She went to check on Max but they'd sedated him so she called Stevens and he drove her home. Tomorrow would be soon enough to find out what went wrong.

Christine woke up early feeling guilty about the way she treated Max yesterday. They'd agreed to live together so he did have a right to know where she was sleeping if she wasn't home...she guessed. She also might have been acting all crazy because of the sex they had and not necessarily...she picked up her phone and checked to see if she had any messages. That was when she saw the missed call from Martha. She frowned at it, wondering why her grandmother would be calling her at midnight. She crept out of her bed and went over to her grandmother's room with trepidation in every step. What if something had happened to her and *someone else* had called to inform her and she hadn't heard the phone? She knocked softly and opened the door; peeking in the room to see that her grandmother was fast asleep. She heaved a huge sigh of relief, watching her, waiting to see if she would wake. When she didn't, Christine decided to go rustle up some coffee, maybe some dry toast to start the day. Whatever she did, she hadn't yet managed to stop herself from puking but hope sprang eternal.

She picked up her phone again and dialed Max' number to apologize. His phone went directly to voice mail and she left a message telling him she would see him later and she was sorry about the whole rude thing the night before. She took a cup of coffee to her grandmother hoping to get the 411 on why she was calling her at midnight. The smell of the coffee seemed to have woken her and she was sitting up in bed, reading her morning verse. Every morning she read a verse from the bible and said her morning prayers before getting up. It had been her habit to do so as a family but then as Christine became an adult and got her own schedule which didn't necessarily gel with Martha's, she'd been leaving it to Christine to find her own time to say her prayers. She looked up now at the rattle of the coffee cup on its saucer as Christine came in the door. Martha smiled at her and motioned for her to come in. Christine put the cup down on the bedside table and sat on the bed as Martha began to read out loud from the chapter.

"Love is patient and kind; love does not envy or boast; it is not arrogant or rude. It does not insist on its own way; it is not irritable or resentful; it does not rejoice at wrongdoing, but rejoices with the truth. Love bears all things, believes all things, hopes all things, endures all things," Martha read.

"What chapter is that?" Christine asked.

"1 Corinthians chapter 13:4-7," Martha said.

Christine nodded her head looking at Martha.

"Let us pray," Martha said and Christine bowed her head.

"Dear Lord, thank you so much for another day of life on Earth.

Thank you for another beautiful sunrise to enjoy. Thank you for the wonderful sounds of nature, from the cool breeze brushing through the trees to the birds singing melodies. You are a wonderful God, full of grace and mercy. I praise you for allowing me another day to spend with my family. I love you Father! Amen," Martha prayed and then opened the bible to another page and intoned "The flowers appear on the earth, the time of singing has come, and the voice of the turtledove is heard in our land."

"That's a beautiful way to start the day gra. Thank you," Christine said.

Martha nodded her head in acknowledgment. "Max needs you; he's in the hospital," she said.

"What?!?" Christine exclaimed dropping the cup of coffee she'd picked up to drink. Martha watched the coffee spread all over her lovely rug and Christine jumped up quickly.

"I'll clean it right up," she said rushing out to get a cloth to mop it up. She brought lots of paper towels to absorb the stains and then wiped it down with a wet towel. She then got a bucket with some soapy water and wiped up any remnants of the stain, really putting her back into it. By the time she was through, she felt better able to continue the interrupted conversation. Her grandmother had gone to the bathroom to clean up for the day so she had to wait for her to come back.

"Gra, what happened?" she asked trying to still the rapid beating of her heart.

"I don't know. It's the sickness. They were doing tests when I left; wouldn't let me see him. They'll let *you* see him – you're his fiancé."

"Did he pass out? What happened?"

"Same thing as last time. Just collapsed on the floor but he managed to hit the call button before he blacked out and Craddock heard him. He was still up luckily, doing the menu for the dinner party Max was planning to have this weekend. He called me; I had just retired – Max asked me to stay over since we stayed late talking. He was worried about you."

"Why was he worried about me?" Christine asked in disbelief and then held up her hand. "Never mind that; we should go to the hospital."

"Yes," Martha agreed. "So leave the room so I can dress."

Christine left the room digging out her phone to redial Max' number again. She was surprised at how hard her heart was beating; how her hands were cold and clammy and sweaty and she had this dizziness in her head. She was worried *sick*...about Max! Fuck, she absolutely did not need this.

The call went straight to voicemail and she left a long agitated message about how pissed off she was that he was sick again and would he not do this to her and his baby; he needed to have more consideration and just not get sick...

Then she tried to call back and erase the message but of course she couldn't. So she called Andrea to maybe get her to do it; she probably had his phone anyway; but she wasn't picking up either. Nobody was answering her! How inconsiderate could they all be anyway? Bloody bitches; Christine could feel herself getting more and more nauseous by the minute. She ran to the bathroom to get rid of the toast and coffee she'd just eaten. By the time she'd cleaned herself up and left the bathroom her grandmother was ready and they left for the hospital.

The nurses claimed that visiting hours weren't for at least an hour but in her status as closest kin got them a face to face with the doctor at least. She let them know what had happened was a relapse situation and that the inflammation was back. Its progress had been insidious and that's why Max had not felt any symptoms before collapsing last night. He would have to be on intravenous antibiotics as well as other intravenous drugs and dialysis to ensure that his kidneys were properly detoxified. He would be out of commission for at least two weeks and sedated for much of that time. With all that said, the doctors were of the opinion that there was no need to hang about the hospital. Christine and Martha insisted anyway. They wanted to be around because Max had asked specifically for Christine last night. The doctor had no choice but to give her permission because stress was bad for the patient.

Max was awake when they walked into his room and smiled faintly as he saw them.

"Hey," he said very hoarsely and Christine hurried forward and picked up his hand.

"Don't talk," she said.

Max opened his mouth to reply and Christine promptly put her hand atop it to stop him.

"I said don't talk," she repeated.

Max closed his mouth.

"The doctor gave us a run down of everything that's wrong with you. Please tell me you haven't been in pain and covering it up all this time."

Max shook his head, his eyes on hers.

"Okay good. So how about you rest, for today, without talking. I'm just going to sit right in this chair and read. We both won't talk. Okay?" Christine said matching actions to words and flopping down into the chair. Martha smiled at them both.

"I'll get you some food. You didn't eat this morning," she said to Christine prompting Max to glare and Christine to look at her with a betrayed look on her face and a shake of her head.

"Always with the big mouth gra," she said chidingly.

Martha just laughed and left the room. Max turned his head to glare at her more intently and she stuck out her tongue at him.

"Oh don't act all high and mighty like you've never done anything wrong in your life. Besides I tried to have breakfast; it didn't take," she said. Max held his hand out to her and she moved her chair nearer to the bed so she could take it.

"I'm glad you're here," he croaked.

"Don't talk," Christine replied.

*****

Andrea took the opportunity to call Claire Lestrange now that there was technically no close kin around. She could justify it perfectly well to Max if he asked by the fact that he'd be out of commission for two weeks and someone needed to be around who could make the decisions if something happened. Someone who was known to all the key players and not some interloper that was claiming to be his fiancée. Not that she would tell him the latter part; she could just keep that to herself. She might also just drop the titbit that there *was* an interloper in case Claire was interested in that little bit of news.

She was on the first flight out of Paris.

*****

Christine's back was killing her. These hospital chairs were really not made for pregnant women to sit on for long periods of time. The wood was hard and the cushion was thin and the back didn't quite bend in a way that accommodated her spine. She wasn't even *that* pregnant; she wasn't sure she should ache this much but she'd hardly moved from her position all day and that could be why. Max slept fitfully all day; when he was awake he tried to talk to her but then she'd threaten to leave if he did so he shut up. But he stared at her with expressive eyes that seemed to really want to make sure she stayed. So she did. Martha came by bearing food at lunch time and stinted Christine for a while as she went to sit in the hospital garden and get some fresh air. She wondered how many more family emergencies she had before she ate up all her days off. Thankfully maternity leave was not affected by other types of days off. But Max really had to stop getting sick; she didn't think she could stand the worry on top of the hyper-acidity of being pregnant. She checked her messages as she strolled about but no one had texted her to protest or to tell her about how the supervisor was complaining. That was always a plus. She really could eat some burritos right about now though. She looked around for a food kiosk where she might get some but couldn't really see any.

She picked up her phone to call her grandmother. "Gra I'm just off to get some burritos, I'll be back later."

"Cravings?" Martha asked.

"Yeah. You want anything from Walmart?"

"I'm good thanks," Martha said in amusement.

When Christine came back to the hospital she found her way to Max' room barred by a huge burly gentleman who claimed to be his body guard. Seeing as she'd never seen him in her life before she highly doubted that.

"I'm sorry but if you don't move right this instant I'll have you thrown out of the hospital for being an imposter", she growled at him. He hesitated a moment but then stood his ground.

"I am commanded not to let anyone through to this room that is not authorized," he said.

"Authorized by whom?" Christine asked trying to walk around him.

"Ms. Claire," the bodyguard said and Christine froze.

"Max' mother is here," she said like a question but more of a statement.

"Yes," the bodyguard replied.

Christine looked up at him. "Where is she?" she asked.

The bodyguard inclined his head to indicate the room. Christine turned her head and saw Martha hurrying toward her shaking her head.

"What?" she asked her grandmother.

"Let's go. I'll tell you on the way," Martha said hooking her arm and dragging her off.

"But...I wanted to see Max-" Christine began to protest.

"Let's not cause a scene in the hospital okay?" Martha said. Christine sighed in an annoyed way and followed her.

They had left the building before Martha opened her mouth again. "Claire is here; she has asked the hospital to ban anyone she does not authorize from seeing Max. She's trying to get Clarence to get him to sign power of attorney over to her. You saw the condition Max was in last night – we don't want to add to that. So we're going home."

"Who the fuck does that woman think she is?" Christine exclaimed.

"His mother. And his closest kin. We're not going to put up a fuss."

"Okay then," Christine said as Stevens drew up. He got out and opened the back door for them and then drove them to Max' place.

"I thought we were going home," Christine said.

"This *is* your home," Martha replied alighting from the vehicle and walking into the building. Christine shrugged inwardly and followed her wondering where this whole mess was going to end up. Max despised his mother; he was going to be so pissed she was trying to take over like this. And that could just not be good for his health.

She followed her grandmother upstairs and went to her room, slumping on the bed and luxuriating at the softness. Her back was profoundly grateful. She could hear her grandmother pottering about in the kitchen, talking to Craddock and the day maid; her name escaped Christine for a minute; she was relatively new to the establishment. She figured she'd have to get to know all the staff's names and what not but not yet...gawd, not yet.

Martha padded into the room holding a steaming mug of something.

"I brought you some hot chocolate," she said.

"Oh, thank you gra, that is very considerate of you."

"Are you having any other cravings?" Martha asked.

Christine thought about it. "No, I think I'm good," she said. "I'll just have a wash and go to bed if you don't mind. It's been a long two days."

"Yes of course, I'm sure you're tired. I'll be in the guest room down the hall if you need me."

"Okay gra, thanks," Christine said already divesting herself of her clothes in preparation for her shower.

*****

Christine started awake in the middle of the night leaning over to the bedside table to check the time and seeing that it was three am.

"Wonderful," she grumbled wondering what she was going to do till morning. She was so wide awake there was no way that she could go back to sleep. She padded to the kitchen to make herself some hot milk and then decided to call the hospital to see how Max was doing.

"Beth Israel Hospital," the voice said on the line.

"Hello, I'd like to check on a patient?"

"What is the patient's name and what is your relationship to the patient?"

"The patient is named Max Lestrange and I'm his fiancée Christine."

There was silence on the other end for a bit.

"Oh, Max Lestrange. He's in a private room and currently awake. Would you like to speak with him?"

"Yes please," Christine said in utter relief. She was supremely surprised that Max was awake at 3am and the nurse was willing to let her talk to him but she wasn't sweating the details.

"Hello," his croaky voice came on the line.

"Max! Gawd I've been worried. How you doing?"

"Great. You didn't come back," he said.

"Your mother kind of banned us from seeing you," Christine said.

"What?" Max croaked. Christine could tell he wanted to shout but had no voice.

"Your mother. She has you on lockdown. She's trying to get power of attorney."

"And you just rolled over and let her?" Max asked in disbelief.

"Well...no. But I wasn't about to get in a street brawl with the burly bodyguard she'd placed outside your door. I didn't think you'd appreciate it."

"Yeah, I wouldn't have. The baby might have been hurt. Will you be by later? I'll take care of the tool at the door."

"Yeah of course we will."

"Why are you awake in the middle of the night? Worried about me?" Christine could hear the smugness seeping down the line.

"Nope. I just slept really early. Could you ask them to let me in to see you around 7am? I have to go to work tomorrow. I mean... today."

"Okay if you say so. Now go get a little more rest if you're working today."

"Yes master."

"Oh, I love when you talk dirty."

"You get some sleep too."

"Yeah, I'll try. The pain is a pain in the arse."

"Can't you ask for more painkillers?"

"I could but I'm tired of being asleep. And groggy. And apparently missing things."

"Nothing really important."

"Yeah, just my mother trying to take over my life before I'm even dead."

"Don't. Don't even say it."

"Say what? Dead?"

Christine's silence was eloquent.

"Okay okay, I'm sorry. How are you feeling by the way?"

"I'm great. The nausea is kicking my ass but other than that…"

"And did you get to the bottom of who's trying to blackmail me?"

"I think so. I got my cousins to work on getting a confirmation that it's really who we think it is."

"And who do you think it is?"

Christine debated with herself, wondering whether to tell him or not.

"Chris…? Come on are we family or not?"

"I don't know about family…when did we become that?"

"When we mixed our blood and bone together and made a new human being?"

"Very evocative imagery. We think it's my mother and her boyfriend husband."

"Hmm."

"Is that all you have to say? Hmm?"

"What do you want to do about it?"

"I don't know. Hit her over the head with Mjolnir?"

"I don't really know where we can get Thor's hammer."

"Warner Bros?"

Max croaked a laugh.

"Yeah I'll make a phone call," he said fondly amused.

"Great. I'm gonna let you sleep now."

"Okay, I'm gonna let you sleep too."

"Goodnight."

"See you at 7am?"

"Yes."

"Okay Goodnight."

Christine hung up smiling at nothing and then padded off to bed, forgetting her milk on the kitchen counter. She started awake at six am and that was how she knew she'd fallen asleep again. She showered, puked and dressed as fast as she could, resolving to get a coffee and a donut from Starbucks on her way to the hospital and thus kill two birds with one stone. She made it to the hospital by seven and the body guard was gone from Max' door. He was awake and sitting up in bed, reading the day's paper.

"Well, you look well," she said placing one coffee cup on the bedside table next to him.

Max looked her up and down. "You look good too. Did you get more sleep?"

"Yes I did. You?"

"Yes," he said folding the paper.

"Liar," Christine said sitting down on the hard chair. "You need a new chair for your guests. This one is hostile," she said.

"I'll have Andrea take care of that right away," Max said smiling as he sipped his coffee.

"Are you allowed that by the way?"

"Allowed what? Coffee? Who cares? I'm drinking it," he said sipping again.

"So. Mother dearest."

"Yeah."

"Plan?"

"Send her back to Paris with her tail between her legs?"

"You're not well enough for a knock down drag out."

"Who said anything about fighting?" Max asked with a smug smile on his face.

Christine narrowed her eyes at him.

Chapter 10

"We've been outed," Cordelia said shaking Kevin awake.

Kevin groaned in response and tried to move away from her hand. She just followed him and tried to shake him into wakefulness again.

"What C?" Kevin said at last, irritably.

"They know it's us wanting to sell their story to the tabloids Kevin, what are we gonna do?"

"It could be anyone; there's no proof it's us."

"The circle is too small; and we're the only ones in it without jobs. Sadie has her online shop, Angie has her hair salon and Aisha is doing her masters. They all have income they can rely on. It's definitely not Andrew cause he has his auto shop that's doing well and Carl's an EMT whose biggest expense is his half of the rent in that big old house he shares with his "roommate" slash boyfriend; and I suspect he don't even pay no rent coz that guy owns half the city and he's gone over Carl. I don't know why they just don't get married. It's legal in Boston and nobody cares that he's gay."

"He cares apparently," Kevin said.

"He must know that we know," Cordelia said thoughtfully.

"Digress much?" Kevin reminded her of her original worry.

"Yes, so I think we need to talk to Mr. Cosby and see how being busted is going to affect our bid."

"Okay If you like. You wanna call him or shall I?"

*****

Mr. Cosby ushered them into his dingy office and then sat down, looking at them expectantly.

"So do you have more titbits for me or...?"

"No, the thing is, I think my family found out that it was us that were going to sell the story. So I'm thinking maybe we should take a step back for now."

Mr. Cosby looked at her intently. "Hey, Ms. Richards it's your decision but do you really want to give up the possibility of a huge pay day just because a member of your family may have discovered that it's you selling the story? Sooner or later, it'll come out. So why not profit from it? Who are you hurting really?"

Cordelia's face twisted in anguish as she thought about it, "I don't know sir, my daughter is pregnant. I don't know if this is gonna cause her a lot of stress but I don't know if I should risk it. If anything should happen to her..."

"What could happen?" Mr. Cosby said. "She has access to the best health care in the city, the best doctors. You said she's living with him right? She's living in the lap of luxury, why would anything happen to her?"

Cordelia's face softened but she still looked troubled. "She seemed very distressed about the news getting out..." she tried again.

"Of course, nobody likes their business in the streets; but don't you think she's being just a little bit selfish? She has this rich man who has to pay child support for the next eighteen years and she begrudges you *one* pay day? Does that seem fair to you?" Mr. Cosby said reaching out to envelope Cordelia's hand in his.

Cordelia shook her head and then nodded it and then shook it again. "I don't know," she wailed.

"It's a good deal," Mr. Cosby wheedled.

"I know it is. I just...I don't wanna like...lose them over this."

"You won't lose them. Why would you lose them? You're trying to make some money of your own. They can't hate on your hustle."

"They actually can," Cordelia said wryly.

"They don't have to know and there will be no way they could prove it. Trust me. I got your back."

Cordelia sat...lost in thought for a long while. Then she sighed and shook her head. "I can't do it," she said standing up. "Call it off."

She walked out of the room, clearly expecting Kevin to follow.

Kevin stood up facing Mr. Cosby, "Go on with the deal. You're right; ain't nobody got the right to hate on our hustle. I'll handle C," he said as he left the room. Mr. Cosby nodded his agreement.

*****

Claire Lestrange arrived at the hospital at 11am to see her son. She had his lawyer trailing in her wake because she needed to persuade him to sign over power of attorney to her. He had come willingly enough when she explained what she needed but she wasn't sure he would back her up in her demands. Still it was a good sign he was here. The bodyguard she'd left outside Max' door wasn't though and that was not a good sign.

Max was still asleep when they walked into the room, just as he had been for every visit she'd made. She turned to Clarence with a significant glance but he was looking at Max and didn't see her. She turned back to her son and his eyes were open.

"Oh," Claire said startled.

"Hello mother," Max said.

"Max," Claire said a bit breathlessly. "You're awake."

"Yes I am. Is that too disappointing?" Max asked.

"Don't be ridiculous Max, of course I'm happy if you're feeling better," she said.

"Mmhmm," Max said sounding extremely skeptical of her. He turned to Clarence. "Good morning sir. Do you have my pre-nup ready?" he asked.

"Pre-nup?" Claire exclaimed.

Max ignored her and continued to look at Clarence waiting for his answer. Clarence rolled his eyes and pulled a document out of his briefcase.

"I have a preliminary draft here for you to look over. I think it covers all the points. Now legally, we cannot include custody issues in a pre-nup-" Clarence stopped abruptly and stared at Claire. "Er, perhaps we should discuss this later."

"Yes, absolutely, you're right. So mother, it's nice to see you but I'm fine. It's not really necessary to be here. You can go back to Paris with absolute peace of mind."

"Don't be silly chérie, I'm going to be here until you are all well," she said. Max sighed deeply, leaning his head back on the bedstead.

"Clarence, could you come back later please. It looks like I'll be visiting with my mother at this time."

"Wait no Clarence needs to stay; we have to discuss power of

www.SaucyRomanceBooks.com/RomanceBooks

attorney."

Max stared at her for a good ten minutes. "I beg your pardon?" he said.

"You're very ill Max and you need to put someone in charge in case something happens to you. As your closest kin it's my responsibility to make sure that happens. That's why Clarence is here; to write a power of attorney for *moi*."

Max and Clarence stared at each other as if to say 'can you believe her?' but neither said a word.

"I already have somebody designated as in charge if something happens to me. Thank you though mother-"

"Somebody else?" Claire screeched. "Who is more qualified than me?"

"My wife to be," Max said resigned to having to tell her now.

"Your...wife to be? I had not heard you were engaged."

"I am," Max said.

"Who is the lucky *mademoiselle* then?" she asked.

"You've met her grandmother; Martha," Max said.

"Your *housekeeper*?" Claire said incredulously.

"Yes," Max replied impassively.

"Have you lost your mind. Insensé!"

"Mother, I don't really have the time or energy for your hysterics right now. Would you kindly leave us?"

"Well...I never," Claire said tossing her head back and stalking out. Max rolled his eyes.

"So you were saying Clarence..." he said with a sigh, settling himself into the bed. "And you can find out when we can leave this dump?"

"Not for another two weeks and nobody's trying to bend that rule Max; you're staying here the entire time; no questions, no negotiations."

Max gave him a betrayed look. "Who died and made you the boss?" he snarked.

"You did. You're going to get well this time Max – you have a kid now. You wanna live to see it or not?"

"Low blow Clarence," Max complained.

Clarence shrugged, "Whatever it takes."

"About the prenup…?" Max reminded him.

"Ah yes, well the arrangements about the baby and the prenup are two separate issues and cannot be in the same contract. I have a standard prenuptial agreement here; division of assets before and after the marriage, the marriage settlement in case of dissolution – I put it at ten million but of course that's subject to change if you disagree – and a list of assets that pre-date the marriage. Does Christine have any assets I need to know of?"

"I'll ask," Max said with a smile.

"What's funny?" Clarence wanted to know.

Max shrugged, "I'm getting married; that doesn't sound funny to you?"

"Sure it does. In fact, I've been tempted to think maybe you lost your mind but you seem fairly sane in spite of what your mama said."

"Not just sane Clarence," Max said, black eyes fixed on him, "Happy."

"Yeah. I see that too."

*****

Claire Lestrange left the hospital in very much of a huff. She was flabbergasted at Max' news. She had gotten complacent in recent years as time passed and Max had stayed single. In his late twenties and early thirties she had been worried he'd find some sweet young thing who would turn his head and give him a couple of kids to dote on. For one thing, she wasn't old enough to be a grandmother, for another, children would play havoc with her game plan to be the sole heir to the Lestrange fortune. Also if Max had kids, he probably wouldn't spend so much of his money on her. She could not allow this; really with the cost of living what it was these days, a drop in income was just not an option. She had to do something...but what? She fished out her phone to call Andrea who had clued her in to what was happening in the first place.

"Andrea? Can we meet for lunch?" she asked.

"Sure. Where would you like to meet?" Andrea asked.

"The Ritz Carlton; bring one of Max's black cards would you?" she said.

"Of course. I'll just run it by him first in case he thinks I'm stealing from him," Andrea said with a laugh.

"I'd prefer he didn't know about this lunch," Claire said a bit coldly.

Andrea was torn; on the one hand she wanted to snap at Claire and ask her if maybe she'd make up her mind whether she wanted to have a secret lunch or if she wanted her son to pay for it. She can't have her cake and eat it. On the other hand, she needed Claire's help in getting rid of Christine...there was always the corporate card after all; and Andrea could report the expense to accounting instead of to Max directly. Even if he eventually found out about their lunch it would not be soon. Short term goals vs. long term goals.

"Okay I understand Mrs. Lestrange," she said.

"Good," Claire said sounding pleased.

They met at 1pm and Claire wasted no time in getting down to business; after she'd ordered some chilled champagne and caviar off the menu.

"Who is this Christine girl and where did she come from?" she asked.

Andrea shrugged. "She's kind of always been around since her grandmother is in charge of the household. She and Max have been…I don't know acquaintances? Friends? I don't exactly know what to call them but you know how Max looks up to Martha so he kind of always felt a responsibility for the granddaughter. He went to her aborted wedding and everything."

"Aborted wedding?" Claire asked perking up.

"Yes. She was going to marry some guy she met in college but it turned out some other girl had prior claim. It was messy," Andrea said with an amused smile. "Max whisked them off to an island in the Caribbean for three weeks."

"Just the two of them?" Claire asked in surprise.

"No. They went with the grandmother too. They were trying to get her to forget about the guy. She was pretty cut up. I thought she still was according to the grapevine. Then suddenly she up and links up with Max and they're having a baby."

"When did this happen?"

"Just after he collapsed the first time," Andrea said fingers steepled and head resting on her hands.

"I get why she would want to have his baby but why would he want to have a child with her? What's so special about her?"

Andrea shrugged. "Like I said he looks up to her grandmother. He treats her more like his mother than..." Andrea looked up remembering who she was talking to. "I'm sorry."

Claire shook her head. "It's okay; I understand. I was maybe not the best mother in the world."

Andrea shook her head and leaned in to cover Claire's hand with hers. "You're still his mother and that means something."

Claire grimaced wryly. "I would hope so...but given that I'm hearing about his impeding marriage and baby from you..."

"There must be a reason he didn't tell you; a reason he doesn't want you to know," Andrea prompted.

Claire thought about it. "He knows she's no good for him," she said.

"So what are you going to do about it?" Andrea asked barely suppressing her glee.

"Tell me about this ex-fiancé. What happened exactly?"

Andrea put her hand up to signal the waiter. She needed some water to get through this conversation. It was going to be a long one.

*****

Clarence walked into Max's room with a bunch of papers.

"We have a winner," he declared prompting Max to turn toward him from his contemplation of the sunset outside the window.

"And who is it?" he asked.

"It's definitely Cordelia Richards and her husband Kevin Brown. The private investigator staked out the lawyer's office and those two were seen leaving there recently. More than once."

"Great, so what's our plan? Are we paying them off?"

"Don't you think that's setting a bad precedent?"

"Okay then, what?"

"I was thinking we could start with mediation; get Martha to speak to her daughter and maybe get her to stop what she's doing."

"If that doesn't work?"

"I have faith in Martha," Clarence said.

"So do I but Cordelia is a bit of a druggie. She might not be thinking straight."

"Yeah yeah I get that. It's still worth a try."

"Fine. I'll talk to Martha and see if she'll do it."

The tread of light footsteps coming down the hall distracted them. They both paused to see who would pass by the door. The footsteps stopped at the door however and they both looked to see who it was.

"Christine," Max called in a pleased voice.

"Hey you," she replied and then saw Clarence. "Oh, am I interrupting business?"

Clarence smiled. "Not at all, in fact we could use your help."

"Oh? How?"

Chapter 11

Christine drove up to her mother's apartment still breathing heavily. The anger was coursing through her veins like bolts of electricity with no grounding. She lunged from the vehicle and dashed into the house banging on the door and calling for her mama.

"Okay okay, hold your horses," her mother said as she opened the door.

"Mama what the fuck are you doing?!?" she screamed not even waiting until her mother had the door closed.

"What am I doing?" her mother asked sounding honestly bewildered; Christine was impressed with her acting.

"You want some MONEY? Is it MONEY you WANT? I'll give you some. HOW MUCH?" her voice was rising and falling in her agitation. Her hands were shaking so hard she couldn't keep them still and she was slightly dizzy with too much adrenaline.

"Chris! Calm down," Cordelia tried to catch hold of Christine's arm but she ripped her arm out of her mother's hand.

"Oh, now you're concerned about my health," she growled.

"Baby, I admit it okay? I did it; I went to a lawyer to try to get some money. But I stopped it. I did. It's over."

"Oh it's over? Is that your story? Are you sticking to it?"

"It *is* over. I told Mr. Cosby to drop it."

"Oh you did huh? Was that before or after he'd asked for a meeting with Max's lawyer *to discuss terms*?" Christine asked arms crossed to prevent herself from strangling her mother.

Cordelia opened her mouth...and then closed it again; looking genuinely puzzled.

"I didn't ask him to do that," she said. Christine stared at her. She really looked like she was telling the truth.

"Well then if you didn't who did?" she demanded.

Her mother's brow stayed furrowed and her eyes were puzzled yet frantic as if she was looking for a way out. Christine moved closer, glaring at her. Suddenly her brow unfurrowed and she looked...there was no other word for it...crestfallen.

"What mama?" Christine asked.

Cordelia's eyes slid to Kevin who was sitting on the couch watching the game and smoking a blunt. Her eyes grew shiny with moisture.

"Kevin?" she said.

He glanced at her overly casual and lifted his brow, "Yeah?"

"Er, you didn't go behind my back and tell Mr. Cosby to..."

Kevin shrugged. "It's our pay day. I figured you didn't want to be involved that's fine. No reason why the rest of us shouldn't."

Christine wanted to run at him, maybe jump on him and bash his head in. she whirled on her mother.

"This is the trash you call a husband? *This*?" she screeched.

"Hey, you shut your disrespectful mouth bitch," Kevin growled.

Cordelia took the two steps that would bring her to the couch and bitch slapped Kevin so hard there was a hand print left on his light skin cheek. "Don't call my daughter that," she said and then looked extremely surprised at herself. Not as surprised as Christine though.

"Bitch what did you just do?" Kevin snapped holding his cheek and glaring up at Cordelia.

"She just bitch slapped you," Christine said helpfully. "Call Mr. Cosby right now and call this deal off before I sic my grandmother on you... bitch."

Kevin sneered still holding his cheek. "And how you gonna make me?"

Christine marched to the table snatched his phone off it and handed it to him. "Kevin, you do not want to know," she said coldly.

Kevin stared at her then at Cordelia standing next to her and then at his phone. He snatched it up resentfully and dialed the lawyer's number telling him to back off as he was no longer interested in the deal.

"Wonderful," Christine said extracting a paper from her pocket. "Now I'm gonna need you to sign this," she said.

"What is it?" Kevin asked suspiciously.

"It's a non-disclosure agreement that forbids you from selling this story to *anyone* or else you're liable to pay a lot of money."

"I ain't signin that shit," he said grumpily.

"There's fifty thousand dollars in it if you sign now. Offer expires in three minutes. Take it or leave it," Christine growled.

Kevin glared back at her for a few seconds before he snatched up the paper and snapped at Cordelia to hand him a pen. Cordelia glared back at him and then handed him the pen to sign.

"You got one of those for me?" she asked Christine.

"Oh, you afraid he won't share the fifty k with you?"

"I don't want the money, I want to sign the agreement; so you know that I won't snitch on you."

"Oh, you suddenly grew a pair did you?"

"Maybe," Cordelia said looking her in the eye. "Believe it or not, the fact that you're my daughter means something to me." Christine cast an eloquent glance at Kevin and then extracted another sheet of paper from her pocket.

"Sign," she said. "There's 50k for you too if you do."

Cordelia nodded and took the paper. She signed it and handed it back, taking the check that Christine gave her in exchange although she did manage to look shamefaced about it.

"This is my new start Chrissy. I promise," she said.

Christine just snorted. "I'll believe it when I see it," she said snatching up Kevin's form and twirling on her heel to leave. She slammed Kevin's check on the table and walked out.

As soon as she reached the car she fished out her phone to call Clarence.

"It's done," she said.

"Wonderful."

"I'll drop them off at the hospital in the morning; you can pick them up from there."

"That is great. I was sort of hoping you'd manage to pass by the hospital this evening. Max was rather pissed off that you had to leave so soon. He blamed me."

"Aww, poor baby," Christine teased.

"So you'll go?"

"I guess. I haven't had dinner yet; we could eat together."

"Aww how romantic."

"Please. Romance has nothing to do with it. It's called hunger."

"Uh huh..." Clarence said. "Well, goodnight and thank you."

"Goodnight and thank you too."

*****

Christine ordered off the McDonald's menu before going to the hospital. Max was still up, waiting for her it looked like. She unpacked her bags; there were burgers, fries and chicken nuggets as well as salad, fish fingers and two milkshakes.

"Mmmm...smells good," he said.

"I know right. I could eat a horse right now so I hope you're not too hungry. Most of this is mine."

Max laughed, "I think I could live on one pack of fries, and maybe one burger?"

Christine shrugged begrudgingly. "Only if you must," she said handing them over. She sat down in the...new chair; a plush original leather confection that cradled her ass like it was her mother.

"Mmm, love the new furniture," she said.

"I had that brought just for you," he said biting into his burger.

"You are a king among men," she said leaning back and popping fries into her mouth.

"So while I have you here..." he said.

"Uh oh," Christine cut in.

Max glared at her. "Can I finish my sentence?"

"Sure go ahead," she said magnanimously.

"Okay, as I was saying we never talked about...you know; what happened the other night."

"What happened the other night? A lot of things have been

happening, a lot of the time at night so...I'm gonna need specifics."

"The night when we...had sex?"

"Oh that night?"

"Yes, that night."

"What would you like to know?"

"Nothing really. I just wanted to check in with you; how are you feeling about it; would you like a repeat...?"

Christine laughed. "Do you really think you're in any condition to have this conversation?"

"Hey, the spirit is always willing."

"Cool. Well when the flesh catches up we can talk about it again."

"But you'd like to talk about it right?" he persisted.

"Sure."

"Okay good, which brings us to our second order of business."

"Which would be what?"

"Marriage," he said.

"I thought we already had that conversation."

"Yes. But with the complications of maman coming back and trying to muscle her way into a power of attorney I need more security because she's right; something could happen to me. So I think we should get the formalities done with."

"By the formalities you mean the wedding?"

"Yes," Max said.

"How are marriage of conveniences carried out then?"

"I was thinking about getting a judge in here; maybe tomorrow?"

"Wow, that fast?"

"Unless you have a better idea," Max said.

Christine snorted, thinking about her first almost wedding. She'd had this long white dress and the cathedral where they were supposed to wed was decked with flowers and balloons and streamers. The church was full of all their friends and relatives. And then Rudy had walked away from her like she meant nothing. This was probably a better idea.

"Whose gonna be a witness?" she asked.

Max shrugged. "Well Clarence will obviously be here...and I thought...Martha?"

"Sadie, Aisha and Angela will kill me if they're not present."

Max shrugged, "So invite them."

"Uncle Andrew and Carl and grandma Misha too?"

"If you want."

"Yeah I think that's my invitation list."

"Your mother?" Max asked.

Christine shrugged. "I think I'll give her a miss for now," she said with a grimace.

Max laughed. "It's funny that both our mothers will not be present at our nuptials."

"Funny haha? Or funny weird?"

"Both?"

"Yeah. I guess. Anyway so it's decided."

"Yes it is. Great. Tomorrow, you're officially Mrs. Max Lestrange."

"Awkward…" Christine said. "Did I not tell you I'm keeping my maiden name?"

Max laughed in delight.

*****

"You have to at least have a new dress!" Martha protested when Christine gave her the news later that evening.

"Fine, I'll stop off at my lunch time and pick something up."

"You'll stop off at lunch time and pick something up? I don't even know who you are anymore."

Christine laughed. "I'm the one who is disillusioned by the trappings of weddings. Besides this is a marriage of convenience gra; it's better not to get things confused."

"Are you telling me or yourself?"

"Both of us?"

"Fine but you're not picking just any dress up for your wedding, I don't care *what* kind of marriage you think you're going to have. I have just the dress for you."

"Oh? You've been hoarding a wedding dress just for me?"

"Actually, it was *my* wedding dress."

"What?" Christine looked down at her grandmother's substantial bust and then down at her own more modest one.

Her grandmother inclined her head and smiled wryly. "I wasn't always this big you know. In fact you and I were of a size when I was your age."

"Hah, you're right I forgot the picture you have hanging on the wall at home of you and grandpa. You were banging."

Martha glared at her.

"Not that you're not still banging or anything. Just in a different way."

"Wonderful. Now that we've got that sorted, you can come home with me and try it on. If there is any adjustment to be done, I'll do it by tomorrow evening."

"Okay," Christine said wondering if she was going to be wearing some funky fifties dress to her wedding. But she trusted her grandmother; if the dress was unsuitable she wouldn't have offered it.

"Okay then, let's go. I'd like to get some sleep. I have a feeling it's going to be a long day tomorrow."

Martha picked up her handbag and they walked to the door. "You can't take a day off?" she asked.

"No. I don't think that's a good idea. Besides my shift ends at 3pm tomorrow. Plenty of time to change and get to the hospital by 5pm for the ceremony."

Martha laughed. "I'm pretty sure Sadie and Aisha would not agree with you. And Angela would fuss about your hair."

"I've texted her already so she's ready for me at 3 on the dot. We're all meeting at the salon and then heading to the hospital from there. Since Max has booked the rooms on both sides of him for privacy we have plenty of space to pretty up and what not."

"Good. I'll meet you there with your grandma and your uncles."

"Wonderful."

"Is Claire Lestrange coming?" Martha asked.

"Max said no."

"That is great...unfortunate; but great."

"Yes," Christine agreed.

* * * * *

Grandma's wedding dress was a wide pleated 1950s skirt with a v-necked strapless top covered by a small matching jacket. The dress was made to be worn with layers of petticoats to give lift and reached just to mid-calf. It was a lovely off white color embossed with roses in the design. Its petticoats were several layers of net and starched for extra stiffness. The dress was in remarkably good repair, in fact it was very well kept. Christine had just exactly the right strapless heels to go with it. She'd been waiting for an occasion to wear them and here it was. The waist was covered with a huge emerald green sash which tied just below her breasts and therefore created no pressure on her blooming waistline. It was perfect.

"I love it grandma. You are a genius."

"I've been saying so for years haven't I?" she said with a grin.

"Yes you have. And now can we please get some rest?"

"Yes of course. Goodnight baby."

"Goodnight gra."

*****

"We are gathered here to unite these two hearts in the bonds of matrimony which is an honorable estate. Into this, these two now come to be joined. If anyone present can show just and legal cause why they may not be joined, let them speak now or forever hold their peace" the celebrant said.

It was too much like déjà vu. Christine tensed waiting for something to happen but everyone just stood around smiling at each other as Max sat on the bed holding her hand. The judge looked down at his book.

"Max Anthony Lestrange, will you have this woman as your lawful wedded partner, to live together in the estate of matrimony? Will you love her, honor her, comfort her, and keep her in sickness and in health; forsaking all others, be true to her as long as you both shall live?" he asked.

"I will," Max said with a smile and a squeeze of Christine's hands.

"Christine Alexandre Richards, will you have this man as your lawful wedded partner, to live together in the estate of matrimony? Will you love him, honor him, comfort him, and keep him in sickness and in health; forsaking all others, be true to him as long as you both shall live?" he asked.

"I will," Christine replied with a curious sigh of relief. She was glad they'd managed to say their vows without...mishap.

"Do you have the rings?" the judge asked. Clarence came forward with a small black box and opened it. Two identical platinum rings inlaid with blue diamonds lay on the velvet pillow.

"Behold the symbol of wedlock. The perfect circle of love, the unbroken union of these souls united here today. May you both remain faithful to this symbol of true love. Please join hands and repeat after me," the celebrant said.

"I, Max Anthony Lestrange do take you, Christine Alexandre Richards, as my wedded partner, to have and to hold from this day forward, for better or for worse, for richer or for poorer, in sickness and in health, to love and to cherish, till death do us part."

The celebrant then turned to Christine and gestured to her to follow his lead.

"I, Christine Alexandre Richards, do take you, Max Anthony Lestrange, as my wedded partner, to have and to hold from this day forward, for better or for worse, for richer or for poorer, in sickness and in health, to love and to cherish, till death do us part."

"For as much as Christine Alexandre Richards and Max Anthony Lestrange have consented together in wedlock, and have witnessed the same before this company of friends and family, and have given and pledged their promises to each other, and have declared the same by giving and receiving a ring, and by joining hands. By the authority vested in me by the State of Massachusetts, I pronounce this couple to be united in marriage. You may kiss," the judge said with a pleased beam.

Max looked up at her and she looked down at him. They both burst out laughing and then Christine leaned down to peck him on the lips. When her lips touched his, he opened his mouth and let her in and what was meant to be a quick acknowledgment of the end of the ceremony became an experimental exploration with 'to be continued' in the subtext. Christine pulled away, cheeks hot, staring at no-one but Max as her family cat called and wolf whistled until a nurse came hurrying in exhorting them to keep it down. Christine found that she couldn't stop looking at Max and he looked right back at her.

"Congratulations Mrs. Lestrange," he said to her.

"Richards-Lestrange," Christine corrected.

"Aha, so you *will* take my name?"

"It's only polite to hyphenate. Everyone knows that."

Max laughed and laughed and laughed.

Andrea had been tasked with bringing in the champagne at this time and she did so, trying her best to look pleased. Everyone toasted save the bride and groom who were both off alcohol for health reasons.

Uncle Carl's "roommate", Sean, who was an amateur photographer took pictures and the celebrations might have continued well into the night if the nurse hadn't come in after half an hour to shoo everyone away.

"We're newly weds, you can't make my wife go!" Max protested.

"Fine. The wife stays but everyone else needs to get out of here. There are other patients who need their rest."

That was the cue for everyone to chorus their goodbyes and leave in an alcohol fueled haze of delight.

"We're so happy for you. Be happy," Sadie whispered as she kissed Christine on the cheek before filing out with the rest. Christine waved at them as they left and then turned back to her new husband.

"Well...looks like it's just you and me kid," she said.

Chapter 12

Christine got home the next day, still wearing her string of pearls and earrings that Max had presented her with just before their wedding. They were her something new. Her wedding dress had been her something old as well as something borrowed, and the blue diamonds on her wedding ring were her something blue. She looked at it, still unable to believe it was real. She was married. Her name was hyphenated. She could audition for real housewives of Massachusetts if she wanted; or Stepford wives or even first wives club...though she didn't anticipate getting divorced. Maybe if Max fell in love with someone...Christine dismissed that thought because she didn't want to think about it. He'd made a commitment and so had she. She knew they would both try their level best to keep it.

She opened the front door, accepting congratulations from the doorman on her nuptials. Max had said something about putting the announcement in the morning papers. She guessed it was done then. She went up to the apartment, contemplating the prospect of firing her grandmother. She really couldn't visualize how her own grandmother was supposed to be her housekeeper. Max had said something about moving her to the office as head of housekeeping there and she hoped that was done because otherwise she couldn't imagine how awkward things were going to be.

"Gra?" she called as she came in. There was no answer so she went to her room to get out of her jeans and shower. She took her time to luxuriate...as she lay back in the bathtub letting the bath salts tickle her skin and the scent of the candle permeate the room, she wondered if she should move in to Max's room. She'd read a few romances in her day, some beginning with marriages of convenience. Most of those couples retained their own rooms. Most of those couples also were in the eighteenth century so really not the best guide...if one were being real, they had already had sex anyway so maybe Max was expecting...Christine found the whole thing extremely confusing. She emerged from her shower to see that she had three missed calls from an unknown number. Her mind jumped to the hospital and the possibility that something had happened to Max since she'd left him this morning. She quickly hit the call back button, breath suspended in fear.

"Hello Christine," a familiar voice said. The breath she'd been holding completely disappeared.

"R-Ru", was all she could say before she completely ran out of breath.

"Yes it's me. I'm in town and I wondered if we could meet," Rudy said.

"You want to meet? Why?" Christine asked in a whisper, her breathing returning to normal very slowly.

"I think it's time that we talked; don't you?"

Christine just stood there with her mouth open, unable to think coherently in any way.

"Tell you what; I have a suite booked at the Ritz Carlton – why don't you come over here? We can have lunch."

"Is your wife with you?" Christine asked finally.

There was a small silence on the line.

"No. she's not," Rudy said at last. "Please. Christine."

"Did you know *I* got married?" Christine asked.

"I read it in the paper this morning. I figured since you've moved on this would be a good time to make peace."

"Make peace?" Christine asked in disbelief.

"Yes."

Christine hung up the phone. She was in complete shock here. She put on her robe and went to the kitchen making herself a hot cup of chocolate with shaking hands and sparing a moment to wonder at her grandmother's whereabouts. She could hear the sound of movement in the house which meant the day maid was around at least, maybe Craddock too. There was no sign of breakfast though; understandable considering that no one had slept at home the night before. She fished out some baked goods from the bread basket and tried to eat it but she was too upset. Her heart was beating frantically and her face was hot. She was all trembly and her hyper-acidity was burning her up from the inside. She couldn't *believe* him. How could he do this? Just call her out of the blue to 'make peace'...who did that? Seriously who brought up that kid; clearly they'd missed a few lessons in how to treat other human beings! Before she knew what she was doing she grabbed her phone and redialed the number. Rudy picked up on the first ring which is lucky for him because she was not in the mood to be kept waiting.

"I don't believe you, you know," she growled down the line.

"I'm sorry," Rudy said, the first time he's ever said that to her that she could recall and it rendered her speechless for a minute.

"Fine then. What time?" she asked.

"Whenever you're available," he said and she ground her teeth in frustration.

"Fine. Now then. I'll meet you at the Ritz Carlton in an hour."

"Okay," he agreed.

*****

Christine was extremely flustered and she couldn't seem to get herself together. Her purse was MIA and she couldn't find those comfy wedges that give her two more inches of height yet are comfortable to wear. Her good jeans were filthy and the ones that she could find have one leg shorter than the other. She didn't want to wear a skirt or a dress; she wanted jeans! She used up almost the entire hour putting herself together so she had to rush out to get to her appointment in time. Rudy was waiting for her as she entered the restaurant. He didn't look much different. He still had the curly hair cut in a box with a line through the side. He's still well built, still tall as she can see when he stands up to greet her. He's kept himself in good shape; and he looks well and prosperous. Christine was disappointed; she'd been hoping he'd grown old before his time, had a receding hairline and a paunch.

"Hello Christine. It's good to see you," he said with a smile.

Christine steadied her breathing and put a smile on her face. "Hello Rudy. I wish I could say the same."

Rudy just ignored that last part and gestured for her to sit. He sat after her, lifting his hand for the waiter to come over.

"So, congratulations on your wedding," he said to her.

"Thank you," Christine replied, fiddling with her purse strap. It just occurred to her that she had a shift starting at 3pm and she did not know how she would be expected to work in this condition. She could feel the nausea building; she would throw up on him pretty soon if she didn't get to a bathroom.

"Excuse me," she said standing up abruptly and heading for where she thought the ladies should be. Luckily, she literally run into a waiter who pointed out the way. She threw up her entire guts and then cleaned herself up before going back out there to talk to her ex-fiancé.

"So. You have something to say to me? Say it." She said.

Rudy leaned forward to cover her hand with his. "I don't know what I can even say," he said.

It was the hand with her wedding ring he covered and now he was caressing the back of that hand with one finger. "I don't know how I can make it up to you," he said, his voice hypnotic.

Christine stared at his hand, waiting for her heart to begin to accelerate the way that it always did when his hands were on her before. She waited for her stomach to drop and the dizziness to come. None of that happened. In fact, her body did not react at all. This was surprising to her and it took her a moment to assimilate. Rudy took her silence for permission to get even more handsy with her.

"Lets go upstairs," he whispered to her. "Let me show you how much I've missed you."

"What?" Christine managed to get out at last, she pulled her hand out of his grip. "Have you lost your mind?"

Rudy shrugged leaning back in his seat with a wry smile. "It was worth a shot."

"You're a sick, sick man," she growled getting up from her seat. "Lose my number would you?" she said and then walked away. She couldn't believe she kept letting this guy get under her skin. She couldn't believe she had ever loved that piece of shit; let alone contemplated marrying him. Suddenly, Christine was feeling a whole lot more optimistic about the future. What had happened hadn't been her fault; *Rudy* was the douche. For the first time since her aborted wedding day, she felt happy again. She had finally dropped the Rudy baggage from her life.

*****

Rudy watched her storm out of the restaurant. He was feeling faintly regretful that she hadn't been game for some horizontal mamba. Christine might not have been very experienced in the sack when they were together but she had been down to try anything. A very amenable bed partner...teachable. And he had a whole lot of stuff to teach. Being with Nat was great and he knew she was the right woman for him, but being with just one chick was boring; variety was the spice of life after all. He fished out his phone and dialed a number.

"Hello. Yeah, well, the plan didn't quite work out. She didn't bite," he said.

"Never you mind. I had a plan B in place just in case. Thank you for your help. The money will be transferred to your Caymans account before the end of the day," Claire Lestrange said.

"Okay. Thank you. Nice doing business with you."

"Goodbye Mr. Sinclair. Enjoy your visit to Boston," Claire said and then hung up. She called another number immediately after.

"Did you get what you need?" she asked.

"I have some great pictures Mrs. Lestrange."

"Wonderful, send them off right away, to *all* the tabloids."

"Already emailing as we speak."

*****

Christine stopped off at Kentucky Fried Chicken and ordered half the menu. She was suddenly ravenous and she had to be at work in less than two hours. It would surely take her that long to get through all the food on her table so she got down to it with no further preamble.

She felt like singing as she got to work, like she was a thousand pounds lighter even as she was getting bigger physically. She was *very* optimistic about the future.

*****

"*Ma chérie,* how are you feeling today?" his mother asked as she came to kiss him on both cheeks.

"I'm doing great *Maman,* and you?" Max replied with a grin. He was almost buoyant with happiness; even his mother's visit couldn't get him down.

Claire gave a shrug. "I am alright. I feel sad that you're here in a hospital bed, hurting and in pain. It hurts my heart," she said with a dramatic hand over said organ.

Max smiled. "I'm sorry I've hurt you mother. But I should be better soon and back home. I feel perfectly fine actually."

"Oh?" Claire asked in concern.

"Yes. I am great."

"Alright then if you are feeling great then how about telling me what is the meaning of this?" she said proffering her iPad forward; it was open on a newspaper article about his marriage. He took it and read it looking up at her finally.

"Yes well, Christine and I were married yesterday, we saw no need to wait. In fact, it was something that you said which made me see that the sooner the better."

"What did I say?" Claire asked genuinely surprised.

"You said that I need a clear line of succession in case something happens to me."

"But…" Claire said her mouth moving like a fish before she found something she could say. "You said nothing would happen to you."

"I did. And I have no intention of checking out now. But I do still have a responsibility and I thought the sooner I fulfill it the better."

"And you are sure that is the right choice? That *she* is the right choice?"

"Yes, I'm sure."

Claire was holding her iPad out again. "So you are fine with your new bride having breakfast with her ex-fiancé the morning after your wedding?" she asked brow furrowed as if she was really puzzled.

Max frowned at her and took her iPad, looking at the article it was opened at.

NEWLY WED CHRISTINE LESTRANGE HAS BREAKFAST DATE WITH MYSTERY MAN

Trouble in paradise already?!? Billionaire Formula One businessman Max Lestrange's new wife was seen this morning at the Ritz Carlton holding hands with a new dude. The guy and Christine appeared to be really cozy and yes people, we know, pictures or it didn't happen right? We happened to get our hands on a few pictures taken on site which clearly show the two holding hands! Whoopsi! Trouble in paradise already?

www.SaucyRomanceBooks.com/RomanceBooks

CLICK HERE FOR PICS

Max found that he was clicking on the link before he had really thought about it. It was a punch in the gut to see that it was indeed Christine sitting there, holding hands with Rudy Sinclair! He stared at the picture as the blood drained from his face.

"Max? Are you okay?" his mother's voice came from afar and he tried to take calming breaths and get rid of her before he completely freaked out.

"I'm fine. Would you excuse me mother?" he asked.

"Yes of course," she said picking up her iPad. Max imagined that he saw a slightly smug smile on her face but he couldn't be sure about that.

He lay back on his pillows. "Right. so…" he murmured to no one in particular. He didn't know how he should feel right now. He wanted to talk to Christine right now, possibly yell at her for meeting with Rudy of all people the *day after* their wedding. Was she sleeping with him? She couldn't be…they had an agreement even if it wasn't a love match; they had shaken on it; no one else but each other. She wouldn't go back on that…would she. Max tried to push it away but she remembered another time that Christine had said she was over Rudy, that she wouldn't see him again; and then had fallen right into bed with him again. But she hadn't been married then...hadn't been pregnant with some other guy's baby. She wouldn't...would she?

"What am I doing believing some stupid tabloid mag?" Max said aloud.

"I don't know, what *are* you doing?" Martha asked strolling into the room and unloading a flask of coffee, some muffins, honey and a fairly large mug.

"Martha," Max says relieved to see her.

"Max," Martha replies.

"Have you moved to the office yet?" Martha asked.

"I don't start till Monday. Meanwhile, I'm trying to find someone suitable to take over for me."

"Have you seen Christine?"

Martha stopped fussing with Max's tea and stared at him.

"I thought she spent the night here," she said.

"She did," Max said staring into the middle distance. "And then she went and had breakfast with Rudy Sinclair."

"What?!?" Martha exclaimed.

Max turned to look at her. "You didn't know?"

Martha frowned. "Who told you that?"

"Pass me my phone," he said and she did so. He clicked onto the URL that the story had been on and handed it to her already opened on the picture. Martha's mouth opened and she looked shocked.

"So you didn't know," Max said watching her.

"Have you spoken to her?" she asked.

"No. I just saw this."

Martha passed the phone back to him, face impassive. "I suggest you talk to her first before going off any deep ends."

"I wasn't planning to go off the deep end," he protested. "I'm just...

surprised."

"I think that you should suspend thinking and concluding until you've talked with Christine."

"Fine. I'll do that."

"Good."

"Pass me my phone."

Martha passes him the phone without a word, pours him some coffee and leaves him alone. Max dials Christine's number waiting for her to pick up without a clear idea of what he's going to say when she does pick up.

"Hey," she answers just as Max was about to hang up.

"Hi," he replies and finds that he can't breathe properly.

"What's up? Are you okay?" she asked sounding concerned. There is no shadow in her words like maybe she's cheating on their one day old marriage...

"I'm..." Max wants to say 'fine' but couldn't quite get the word out, "confused," he says instead.

"Oh? What's up?" Christine sounds very light and happy underneath the concern. Is it because she's seeing her first love behind his back?

"I'm looking at this picture of you," he tries to let her know without mentioning *his* name.

"Aww how sweet, what picture is that?" she asks sounding completely oblivious to even the possibility of wrong doing.

"A picture of you...at the Ritz Carlton. And you're not alone," he says.

There is a short silence.

"Oh," she says at last.

"Oh? Is that all you have to say?"

"This isn't a conversation to have over the phone."

Max's heart drops to his feet. "Just tell me what you were doing there with him. Have you been seeing him this whole time?"

"No!" she exclaims and the surprise in her voice that he would think that seems honest enough.

"Then what then?" he asks. He's almost yelling in his upset.

"He called me this morning wanting to talk. To make peace. I thought it was bloody time so I agreed."

"So that was a smoking the peace pipe type meeting?"

"Yes and no."

"What do you mean yes and no!" his efforts to keep from yelling were quickly falling by the wayside.

"I mean I went there with the intention of...you know, laying that ghost to rest but it turned out he had other intentions so I left."

"Really?"

"Yes. Really."

"Okay then...will I see you later?"

"I'm at work right now and I'll be leaving here late. I thought I'd get some sleep and come see you tomorrow."

The silence was heavy with unsaid things for a moment.

"Okay then I'll see you tomorrow."

"Yeah okay, so...er have a good day."

"You too."

*****

Max was a bit more settled after that phone call but he was also rather perturbed at the level of his upset. He wanted to leave his bed and maybe go and kill Rudy Sinclair. He also wanted to strangle Christine for going to meet with him.

"Your grand daughter will be the death of me," he complained to Martha when she came back into the room.

"Will she now?" Martha said not sounding very concerned.

"Yes. We haven't been married one day and I already want to lock her in the basement," he bit out.

"Oh? I didn't know we had a basement," Martha said packing up the snacks that Max had neglected to eat. "Was the food not to your liking, would you like something else?"

Max just gave her a side long glance. "What? Nothing to say about my potential caveman tactics?"

"How you and Chris conduct your marriage is none o' mine. I learned long ago not to get in the middle of people's marital woes."

Max raised his eyebrows. "Even when they ask you to?" he asked.

"*Especially* when they ask."

Max laughed.

"I'm going to leave you to rest now. Any special requests for your dinner?"

"Something with fish in it; maybe French fries? Some salad."

"Okay then. I'll leave you to rest. Try to get some won't you?"

"Yes mom," Max said with real affection. Martha just smiled as she left.

*****

"I need you to leave," Cordelia told Kevin when she got home that day.

"Leave? Girl watchu mean?"

"I mean to the left baby boy, everything you own in a box to the left," Cordelia pointed. There was actually a suitcase in the corner that seemed to be packed. Kevin had been home all day and hadn't noticed it.

"I hoped you'd take your things and be gone by now but clearly you need to hear the words," she said.

"Where is this coming from baby?" Kevin coaxed standing up and coming toward Cordelia.

"Look you got your fifty grand; could you go blow it somewhere else. I meant what I said to my daughter about turning over a new leaf and clearly you ain't the man to do that with."

"Why not? Why not me? What's wrong with me?"

Cordelia put her hands on her hips and glared at him. "Let me count the ways…" she said and proceeded to break down to him the various ways he'd let her down including going behind her back and telling the lawyer to proceed with Max's extortion when she'd *specifically* nixed that idea.

"So what? So you think you better than me just coz you got cold feet at the last minute? You was just scared they was goin to find you out and cut you off from the fambly. You ain't no better than me so don't be frontin here like you are," he sneered.

"Fine. I'm not better than you. I still want you to go," Cordelia said swiveling her head with attitude and pointing to the door. She could see Kevin wanting to argue further but she just gestured again for him to leave and that shut him up. He walked to the suitcase and picked it up and then looked at her again.

"Where am I supposed to go?" he asked sounding heart broken.

"Call Tyrone. How the fuck should I know. I look like your mama?" Cordelia asked holding the door open for him.

Kevin inclined his head. "You'll be calling me when you lonely. Don't expect me to pick up," he said as he walked past her.

"Uh huh. Whatever you have to tell yourself boo boo," Cordelia said and closed the door firmly behind him. She had fifty grand and her daughter had just married a billionaire. It was time she was done with the hood rats.

*****

Max would have gotten some sleep; in fact he had fully been intending to – but his phone was switched on and apparently everyone in Massachusetts had seen both his marriage announcement and the story about Christine meeting some mystery man for breakfast. As a result his phone was ringing all day with people either extending congratulations or trying to find out more details. Worse yet, a tabloid got hold of his number and called him for comment on the story. After that, he switched off the offending device wondering belatedly where Andrea had got to. But even after the phone was off he was too agitated to sleep. He was tired of being at the hospital. He wanted to be home in his bed...with his wife. The word felt strange on his tongue and yet at the same time it fit perfectly. Dr. Benson came around to check him that evening and the first question he asked as soon as he caught sight of him was when he could go home.

"You have four more days Max and then you can go home," he said.

"I feel so much better now Carlyle, can't I check out in the morning? I promise to be on bed rest, *at home*, for as long as you like."

Carlyle laughed and shook his head. "You really are hopeless Max aren't you?" he said fondly.

"Absolutely hopeless. So are we gonna do this or what?" Max said eagerly.

"Let's give it one more day and then I'll check you out. Deal?" Dr. Benson said.

Max leaned back against his pillow in resigned disappointment. "Okay then."

*****

Christine was distracted at work. The phone call from Max was doing all sorts of things to her insides; she did not understand his tone, what was he trying to imply? He surely did not think she went straight from her wedding ceremony to cheating on him with that scum of the earth...I mean...how many years had they known each other? Did he really not know her *at all*? The more she thought about it, the more upset she got. By the time her shift was over at

9pm she knew she couldn't get any sleep until she'd given Max a piece of her mind. Thankfully, her new status as wife gave her a lot more mojo with the hospital so they couldn't just turn her away if she wanted to see him; visiting hours or no. At least she *hoped* so. If she had to get admitted to the hospital to talk to him, that was what she was gonna do. This shit needed to get sorted like yesterday.

She stormed into the clinic and past the nurse at reception who looked up, opened her mouth and then closed it again. The rage that Christine was radiating was palpable and nurse Felicia did not get paid enough to try to get between her and her target. She did call security to be on stand by in case they needed to throw someone out of the ward in a minute. Christine reached Max's room unmolested and found him sitting up in bed, watching CNN.

"Well, and hello there," she said hands on hips as she came into the room. Her face was so hot she had to take off her jacket just to cool off a little.

"Christine!" Max exclaimed in surprise. "I didn't expect to see you today."

"Didn't you?" Christine bit out.

Max frowned. "What's the matter?" he asked straightening up. He didn't know what was happening but instinct told him it was bad. Christine's hair was all over the place and she wasn't wearing any earrings.

"I don't know Max, you tell me. What *is* the matter with you?" she said in a pseudo calm tone.

"Well I have this chiefly undiagnosed prostate complaint other than that I'm not sure..."

"Oh you're not sure?" Christine asked sarcasm dripping from every word. "You're not sure what?"

"I'm not...sure what it was I did to piss you off," he said studying her face closely.

Christine inclined her head to the side, mouth pursed, breathing hard through her mouth. She was trying her best to calm down; she really was. But every time she thought about Max thinking that she was cheating on him *the day after their wedding* with Rudy Sinclair she could literally feel her arteries exploding.

"Why don't you ask me then? Ask me now or forever hold your

peace," she said.

"Ask you what?" Max asked quietly.

"Ask me…if I'm fucking Rudy. Isn't that what you wanted to know this morning?" Christine could barely get the words out.

Max stared at her but didn't say anything.

"Well?" Christine was almost yelling.

"Well, if I thought you were fucking Rudy do you think I'd be lying here calmly watching CNN?"

"Well then why did you ask me that?" Christine asked and now she was definitely yelling.

"I saw a picture of you in the tabloids with an old flame I know you still have feelings for, don't you think I had the right to ask what you were doing with him?" Now it was Max's turn to almost yell. Christine turned away from him and closed the door before swiveling back to glare at him.

"I don't have feelings for him," she said coldly.

"Oh yeah? Since when?" Max asked not bothering to hide the skepticism in his tone.

"Since…today," Christine said quietly. "I realized this morning what a piece of shit he really is."

"Oh you realized that this morning?" Max asked sarcasm dripping from every syllable.

Christine flipped him the bird but came closer to the bed and sank down into her comfortable leather chair. "I don't know how I could have been so blind," she said thoughtfully, mostly to herself.

"Chris, why did you go to meet him?" Max asked. "Why today?"

"I told you, *he* called *me*. All I wanted to do was get some food in me before I got to work and he called and said he was in town and he wanted to meet and congratulated me on my nuptials…it was very confusing. He threw me."

"Was that before or after you realized he was a piece of shit?" Max' tone was striving for even but there was a thrum of anger beneath that was unmistakable. Christine turned her honey brown eyes on him, open, hiding nothing.

"It was before. I went to see him to maybe close the books on that awful chapter in my life. I was ready to hear him ask for forgiveness and maybe give it. Instead, I got sleazy propositions and more of the same. Somehow this time I could see right through the smarmy charm. Do you think I've grown up at last?" she asked with a rueful smile.

"Nah, I think it's my DNA swirling around inside you that saw through him. You're still as dumb as ever," Max said and it was mostly a joke. Christine thumped his arm.

"Ouch! Watch it honey, I'm still a very sick man," he protested.

"And I'm a pregnant woman. So move over so I can get some sleep," she said pushing him.

Max made room for her on his bed and she took off her jeans but left her t-shirt on and climbed in. They spooned quietly just holding on to each other until they both fell asleep.

Chapter 13

Christine woke up to the tickle of Max's finger tracing patterns on her thigh. She lay still, letting him run his hand up and down her naked leg, sometimes getting really close to her ass but never quite touching it and then back down. She could feel the hardness of his erection against her hip and wondered if he wanted to do her right here in the hospital with the possibility of a nurse barging in at any second very real.

"Are you awake?" he murmured into her shoulder. Christine took a deep breath, lifting her shoulder slightly in answer but didn't say anything.

"You smell of honey and sunshine," he said and she giggled.

"Pretty sure I don't," she replied into the pillow. Her whole body was languid with contentment. She felt no bite of morning sickness to mar the beautiful morning so she didn't want to move lest she remind any part of her body that she was actually harboring an alien inside her and it was not happy about it.

"How would you know? You can't smell yourself," he said rubbing his nose against the naked skin of her exposed shoulder. His hand was moving the t-shirt she was wearing out of the way so he could cup her breasts and press his erection more firmly against her.

"How does sunshine smell anyway?" she asked amused against her will.

Max took a deep breath. "Mmmm," he murmured. "Like you."

Christine huffed a laugh. "You are a useless describer," she said. Max's hand came into view as he reached over to turn her so she was facing him.

"I haven't brushed my teeth," she protested weakly.

"Neither have I," he said as his mouth closed over hers. Her lips softened and opened for him, letting his tongue explore at will before she got in on the action and began to kiss him back in earnest.

"Mmmmm," she said, loving the taste of him. "You smell of apples and oranges," she murmured into his mouth with a small laugh. He laughed as well but didn't let that distract him from licking into her mouth and almost lodging in her throat. His body began to undulate as he pressed his erection deeper into her skin. He turned with her again so she was beneath him and pressed her down into the mattress.

She broke away from his lips to whisper, "The nurse could come in at any time."

He lifted his eyebrows at her. "Are we not married? This is crucial for the consummation of our marriage. We're merely obeying the law," he said before nipping at the line of her jawbone and down to her chin.

"And you're sure you're strong enough for this?" she asked even as she inclined her head to give him greater access. He stopped what he was doing to stare into her eyes.

"Why? What are you planning to do to me?" he asked, all eager anticipation. She snorted her amusement and hit him on the shoulder and then pulled his head back so he could continue to eat her shoulder blade. She spread her legs slightly so he was lying in between them and then crossed them around his waist arching upward to let him know she wanted him to...

"You're not one for foreplay are you?" he asked.

"I just want you inside of me now. We can foreplay all you want later," she said impatiently.

"God, you know how many men would kill for a girl like you?" he asked smugly even as he drove home. Christine made an inarticulate sound in response. Max withdrew from her completely and drove into her again, harder. The sound Christine made this time could possibly only be heard by members of the canine family.

"Max," she breathed arching upward to give him greater access and enable him to go deeper. "Want," she said.

"You want...?" he asked as he pounded into her, almost driving her through the mattress.

"More," she finished taking her legs in her hands and pulling them up almost to her face so his access was unimpeded. He got up on his hands and swiveled his hips as he thrust into her. She was making mewling sounds of encouragement, eyes rolling back in her head and hips making uncoordinated arching thrusts of their own, attempting to meet Max as he drove into her. The room was quiet apart from the hard slapping sound of flesh on flesh and the grunts and moans they couldn't quite suppress.

"Oh God, so good," she moaned throwing her head back and letting her legs go because her hands were too weak to keep ahold of them any longer. Her whole body felt languid and weak yet coiled and tense like a cobra about to strike. She needed release and she needed it now but she didn't want this to ever stop.

"Don't ever stop," she said dropping her legs on either side of the bed and pulling Max's face to hers. He took her mouth in his; it wasn't a kiss though, just another way to get inside her. Perhaps he wanted to lick his own penis through her throat. It certainly felt like he was trying. She felt filled at both ends yet there was this part of her that was empty and waiting, striving to reach out to him but unable to quite do it. His hand reached between them and brushed softly against her swollen clitoris, once, twice and then suddenly that space was full, so full it was bursting out and spreading detritus everywhere. Her whole body convulsed upwards, shaking and shuddering and spilling liquid everywhere. There were stars and rainbows where before the hospital ceiling had been and for a moment, only blackness. And then Max began to shudder and shake and moan as if he was in pain. His seed spilled inside her and that caused her to clench upwards, sucking and milking for all she was worth as aftershocks streaked all over her body causing her to tense again as her insides liquefied, again. They came down together, unable to move or speak for a long while.

"Well...I'd say we're officially married," Max said into her collar bone.

"Yeah I would have to agree with that assessment," Christine replied, a satisfied smile curling her lips. "Now get off me before I suffocate."

Max slowly rolled off her, almost toppling off the single bed but Christine reached out to clutch him closer.

"My hero," he said eyes closed, a lazy smile playing on his lips.

*****

The nurse woke them up as she came to check on Max's temperature. She let out a small squeal of surprise as she came through the door which woke Max up. He smiled smugly at her and then followed her horrified eyes to a sleeping Christine in his arms.

"Oh don't mind her. She's just my wife," he whispered. "Was there something you wanted?"

"I need to take your temperature," she whispered back obviously very flustered. The room smelled strongly of sex, and Max was completely unclothed. Luckily the sheet covered all the more interesting parts of their anatomy and Christine's t-shirt was still on...if very askew. Max dug his hand from under Christine's head and then sat up, making sure the sheet was still concealing all his privates.

"Go ahead," he said and she came forward slowly and put the thermometer in his mouth.

"Mr. Lestrange, your wife can't be here," she said blushing deeply.

Max nodded his agreement but pointed at the thermometer to indicate that he couldn't talk. She took it out of his mouth, sooner than she should he suspected and then shook it and looked at the temperature.

"Back to normal," she said with another shy smile, and wrote that down on the chart.

"Great. So I can leave today?" he asked leaning slightly into Christine's shoulder.

"That's up to the doctor," the nurse said and left in a hurry. Max looked down at a still sleeping Christine and smiled. He bet she would have been mortified if she'd been awake for the nurse's visit. He knew he should wake her up; after all, the nurse would soon be followed by a doctor not to mention Martha bearing breakfast. He really *should* wake her…it was just that she looked so peaceful and content. Max's eyes traveled down from her exposed shoulder to the dip of her still slim waist and then the swell of her hips. He found that he wanted to touch her again, to caress, to feel her. Learn the curves of her body like he knew his own, penetrate her deep and mark her so well that everyone would know she was his, and his alone.

Somewhere in the back of his mind he was startled by these Cro Magnon thoughts. When did he become such a cave man? It didn't stop him from placing his hand gently on her hip. He could see the marks of his fingers where he had pressed into her, holding her tight as he pounded her pussy. He was not surprised to find that he was hard again. That he wanted to do it again. His hand trailed her flesh of its own volition, looking for her warm center. He felt detached from it, like it had a mind of its own; it would go where it would without any input from his brain. His other hand closed on her round, plump ass; so shapely…it fit exactly in the palm of his hand. Like it was made for him. He squeezed gently, darting his eyes at her face to see if she woke but her breath continued to go in and out evenly. He ran his finger up and down her gluteal cleft, wondering if he could breach…

Christine's breathing changed suddenly, she took a deep breath and suddenly her eyes were open, and on him. He frowned in puzzlement, wondering when she'd gotten such mesmerizing eyes; they sucked him in with their soft honeyed sweetness and he wanted to drown in them. He must be high.

"Did you roofie me?" he asked.

She laughed in delight, the sound brightening the room inexplicably.

"Hey, you're the one with access to all the drugs," she said. Her voice was deep and low; throaty with sleep. It was doing bad things to his self control.

"Maybe so…but that would mean you're intoxicating me all on your own," he said leaning forward. Her brow furrowed as if she didn't understand what he meant…maybe she didn't but she would pretty soon. His lips closed upon hers. He felt them, tasted them, savored their plump pliability; he sank into them and let them create the dizzying vortex that terrified and elated him in turn. He suspected that he might be bewitched.

*****

Christine watched Max's lips coming toward her. In the back of her mind she knew that this was neither the time nor the place. Max was sick, they were in the hospital...this was a marriage of convenience for God's sake! And convenience did not include having sex whenever it was convenient. It was supposed to mean the opposite of that. Cold, businesslike, unemotional. She was feeling anything but that. Her heartbeat was speeding up just from the hot looks he was giving her; she could feel his hardness against her thigh and all she wanted to do was open wide and let him in. Hell, she didn't even care if the whole fucking hospital knew what they were up to in here. She wanted this in a way that she'd never experienced before. Not with Rudy or with any of the other substitutes she'd sought over the years. This was some new shit and somewhere where her common sense stood guard over her heart, she was terrified. The rest of her was busy yearning toward him; wanting him to fill her emptiness, like now. She thought about him saying that she wasn't one for foreplay. She'd said that they could have that later. As his lips touched hers, she hoped it wasn't later yet. Sure she loved the kissing and the touching, but right now she really needed him to fill her up again; take the emptiness away. Her center was crying out for him, wanting him to come in to the home he'd already carved out inside her and fill it with his presence.

Maybe it was being pregnant that made her feel this way...so *hungry*. Hungry for touch, for taste, for the sound of him moaning loudly in her ear as he gave his body to her; no holds barred. Perhaps *that* was the difference. That was what she was so hungry for. The utter surrender that she felt from him even as he dominated her, surrounded her, and fucked her into the ground – she felt like at that very instant when he was at the apex of his dominion over her, he was also completely hers to do with as she pleased. He was hers, as she was his. It was breathtaking.

*****

"Enough of that you two, you're in a public place now," Martha's voice startled them out of the bubble they'd built around themselves that allowed them to forget where they were.

"Martha!"

"Gra!"

They both said simultaneously as the tried to untangle limbs and arrange bedding so as not to reveal any incriminating details.

"I mean seriously you two; you couldn't wait one day? I just ran into Dr. Benson and he said he's discharging you today," Martha said putting her bag down on the bedside table and looking unperturbed at their perturbation. She began to unload flasks and mugs and containers filled with lovely smelling things and then she turned for the door.

"I'll give you five minutes to straighten yourselves out; I'll just go distract Dr. Benson – he's coming down the hall and he doesn't need to see this," she swept her hand around to cover the bed and them in it as she said 'this' and then she tossed her head and walked out the door, closing it gently behind her.

Christine slumped back on the bed, laughing quietly.

"Well...that just happened," she said regarding Max from beneath her lashes. Max smiled back at her.

"Yeah. So, get dressed?" he asked.

"Yes," Christine said surging up and rooting around beneath the blankets to try to find her t-shirt. Max slid out of bed and picked up his pyjama bottoms from the floor and put it on. He looked around, trying to remember where he'd put his shirt and trying to ignore his straining erection. No one ever died of blue balls after all...he was pretty sure. Christine had found her shirt and put it on so at least her boobs were no longer on display. She jumped out of bed and picked up her jeans from the chair and slung them on, her pretty ass on display for a bit too long for Max's taste.

"Excuse me while I..." he trailed off as he hurried into the bathroom and closed the door behind him. He divested himself of his clothes and stepped into the shower, taking hold of his penis as he did so.

"No fair, jerking off and leaving me high and dry," Christine called as she banged on the door of the bathroom. Max just laughed. He was going to enjoy being married to her.

*****

When Dr. Benson came in, everyone was decent and respectable again, cups of coffee in hand and croissants on plates; having a civilized non-hedonistic breakfast. Martha came in behind him narrowing her eyes at them both as if to say that they did not fool her.

"So Max, how are you feeling this morning?" Dr. Benson asked.

Max grinned widely. "I am on top of the world Carlyle. I'm ready to go home."

"Are you now?" Carlyle said returning the smile. "Well let me see." He proceeded to conduct a thorough examination on Max and then accepted a cup of coffee from Martha as he summed up his findings and gave them advice for care, especially for the remaining three days but also going forward. He gave them all the signs they should watch out for in case of impeding relapse and what to do should they notice this. He also recommended some supplements to take and food groups such as tomatoes to imbibe in order to ensure that his health continued to be good. Lastly, he gave them a check up appointment in two weeks' time.

"Well, I think that's mostly it. I'll sign your check out papers and you can go home," he said grinning at the delight on Max's face.

"Thank you Dr. Benson. I really appreciate everything you're doing for me."

Carlyle put up a hand. "Don't mention it. Its what I'm here for." He turned to Christine, "And you Mrs. Lestrange, how is the baby doing?"

"Please. Call me Christine. And the baby is fine. thank you for asking. We had our first check up a few weeks ago."

"Oh, that is great and your overall health? How are you feeling?"

"Nauseous," Christine said with a smile.

Carlyle grimaced in sympathy. "Only to be expected. Your OB/GYN knows this?"

"Yes I did tell her. She gave me some pills to take if it gets bad."

"What is your doctor's name?" he asked.

"Dr. Mulholland."

"Mm, good doctor. I've heard the name," Dr. Benson said nodding.

"I'm glad you think so," Christine said with a smile. Dr. Benson nodded and then put down his emptied coffee cup.

"Well then, I'll just get that paperwork for you and you'll be home before you know it."

"Thank you doctor," Martha, Christine and Max chorused in unison.

Max smiled at Christine. "I'm coming home," he grinned. There was a definite gleam in his eye.

*****

The question of which room she should sleep in remained unresolved. It was Christine's day off so she was able to go home, air out rooms, get some fresh flowers in and change the sheets on Max's bed. Martha had offered to do it as she still had a few days before she was an employee of Lestrange enterprises and not Max Lestrange, but Christine had promptly informed her that she was so fired and there was no way she was coming to clean the house.

"What if I came as your grandmother and not as housekeeper?"

Christine thought about it, biting her lip. "Nope. You go home, rest up. I got this," she said.

"Okay...but I'm just a phone call away if you need anything," she said.

"Did you get me a replacement housekeeper yet?" Christine asked.

Martha shook her head. "They really is nobody suitable. I don't know if I will get someone," she said. Christine smiled, knowing full well what her grandmother's problem was. Letting go was hard, and maybe it shouldn't be her job to get someone to replace her.

"How about I just call the temp agency for now?" she asked.

"Oh no child, those gals come in, they scope out your home and then they call their thievin' cousins to come steal you out of house and home. You don't want to be messing with no temp."

"Then what?" Christine asked.

Martha put a hand on her shoulder, "Don't worry child, I'll have someone for you by the weekend. You can manage till then right?"

"I guess so," Christine said. She made sure to sound uncertain so her gra wouldn't feel dismissed.

"Good. Now you go on home and get ready for your husband," she said. There might have been a naughty gleam in her eye when she said it, but Christine couldn't be sure.

*****

Max called from downstairs when Stevens brought him home later in the day.

"Is it safe to come up?" he asked.

"I believe so," Christine said.

She waited at the door for him so that when he rang the bell she was right there.

"Did you forget the keys?" she asked eyes shining.

He shrugged. "Hey, the house has a new owner now, I can't just be walking in like I own the place."

Christine smiled. "Oh. Well someone should have informed me because I've been acting like you own the place all day," she said hand on hip.

Max smiled, "Come here."

Christine raised a brow, "Why?"

"Just come here girl," Max kind of growled still standing outside the door. Christine came expecting him to kiss, or touch or hold. She was very surprised when he lifted her up in his arms.

"Oh!" she exclaimed. "Are you sure you should be doing this?" she asked holding on to his shirt as she stepped through the doorway and walked with her toward the bedroom. His hold was surprisingly rock steady for someone who'd been in the hospital not twenty minutes ago.

"Isn't this how a bride is supposed to be carried into her new home?" he asked softly.

Christine just smiled.

Chapter 14

Christine came waddling into the room, her stomach getting there about five minutes before her. Max folded the Financial Times he'd been reading and smiled up at her.

"Good morning ma chère," he said.

"Ma chère my ass. Which is aching just so you know," Christine complained.

Max wrinkled his nose and suppressed a grin, "TMI."

"Ha. No such thing when you're this pregnant. You broke it, you bought it, you share in the pain of what a pain in the ass third trimester pregnancies can be."

"You know there are thousands of women who-" Max began sanctimoniously still trying to suppress the grin.

"I swear if you start up again with that 'thousands of women who would kill to be pregnant' crap again I will kill you. You will be deceased," Christine threatened.

Max put up his hands and cowered laughing. "I'm so scared," he said.

"Oh you better be," Christine said pulling the plate of taquitos toward her. She'd developed a hankering for Mexican food in her last month of pregnancy which was very inconvenient seeing as she was also extremely prone to hyper-acidity. Max stood up, placing the container of cold yogurt next to her as she dug in. It helped with the acidity sometimes, other times she had to resort to antacids, a huge jar of which stood on her other side. Max had tried to persuade her to maybe not eat spicy foods instead of going through this circle of suffering and had almost gotten a blade to his heart as a result. He tended to be much more cautious in his approach these days. She was just pouring herself a large glass of yogurt when she felt a clenching sensation in her lower stomach. She bent forward clutching at it, trying to speak and finding that she couldn't. Max had already left the room; was probably collecting his keys in readiness to leave for work. As she looked frantically around for something to call out with, a phone, anything, her eyes fell on the little silver bell that Craddock had got her. It was supposed to be a joke because she was constantly eating which meant she was constantly wandering over to the kitchen and bumping into everyone and everything. So Craddock had gotten her a bell to ring when she wanted something brought. She'd responded by ringing it every five minutes for the first three days but she'd gotten tired of his never ending patience as he answered it so she'd stopped... unless there was really something she wanted from the kitchen. She grabbed at it now and rang it frantically, hoping for someone to come quickly before she died of pain in her seat. She felt something vital loosen and liquefy and then warm wetness spread down her tights. *Was she bleeding?* Christine was now genuinely terrified.

"What?" Max's languid voice inquired from the doorway and then his tone changed as he saw her hunched over in her seat. "Christine? What's wrong?" he asked urgently hurrying over to shake her by the shoulder. That was not helping and she made an inarticulate sound of protest.

"Craddock! Sarah! Anyone!" Max shouted trying to straighten her up. But that just increased the pain so she resisted. Someone came hurrying into the room in response to the urgency in Max's tone.

"Call an ambulance!" he shouted to whomever it was and they went scurrying off.

"It will be alright baby. What can I do?" he asked trying his best to be reassuring as he rubbed at her back but the fear he was feeling dripped through every word. Christine tried to say something but she was too breathless to speak and the pain was unbearable.

"Sarah! Did you get an ambulance?" Max shouted as he tried to lift Christine out of her seat.

"They said five minutes," Sarah, the day maid said rubbing her hand anxiously as she hovered by the door. "Can I do anything else?" she asked then looked at the wet floor. "I'll just wipe that," she said hurrying off to get a mop.

The ambulance was true to their word and five minutes later they were at the building. Max was outside waiting with Christine in his arms. He had tried to wait but Christine's continued distress got to him so much that he had to feel he was doing *something*. So he carried her down the stairs as she cried steadily.

"Is it supposed to be this bad?" he asked the EMT as they got her on a gurney and placed an oxygen mask on her.

The EMT did not deign to answer, stripping off Christine's tights as the vehicle took off and examining the bloody fluid that surrounded her.

"It's just bloody show, perfectly normal," he said aloud as he took Christine's pulse. Her breath was coming in hitches and she was still trying to bend over double as the EMTs pushed her back to lie flat.

"She's in pain, won't you give her something for that?" Max asked in distress. Christine's eyes were wild and unaware, staring into nothingness as she struggled for breath, her whole body hitching with every intake and lurching with every exhale.

"I can't give her something right now. We need to find out what we're dealing with first," he said.

"She's pregnant; can't you see that?!?" Max asked on the edge of hysteria.

"Sir, I'm going to have to ask you to please calm down. We are doing our level best to ensure that your wife gets the best care possible," the other EMT said looking him in the eye. Max tried to calm down and let them get on with it but it was hard to see her like this and not want to beat somebody to a pulp for letting the pain continue. The ride to the hospital was thankfully a short one and Dr. Mulholland was waiting when they arrived. Max made a mental note to give Sarah a raise for ensuring that the ambulance and Dr.

Mulholland were informed on where to meet them because his brains were scrambled right now. The doctor was right there as the gurney was removed from the ambulance, with Christine still trying her level best to hunch into a tight ball of pain.

"Christine? It's me, Dr. Mulholland. Show me where it hurts," she was saying even as her stethoscope was out and she was touching Christine in various places to see her reaction. The gurney was hurried along past the emergency room and into an OR. A nurse stopped Max at the door stating that there was some paperwork to be done and could he step this way.

"My wife...I need to be with her," Max said resisting her attempts to move him from the door.

"And you will. Just, you need to complete this paperwork and then you can scrub in. It won't take more than a minute or two I promise you Mr. Lestrange."

Thankfully they'd been taken to the fertility center where the staff were familiar with them so it really did not take more than a minute to fill in the forms. Then the nurse was leading him to a scrub room and showing him what to wear and how to wash his hands. He did as he was bid and then he was allowed into the OR where Christine was already sedated.

"Max," Dr. Mulholland said as he stepped in the room, looking up quickly and then back down to her work. "It looks like Christine has suffered something called Placenta Abruptio. We must get the baby out as fast as possible and then stabilize both mother and child. If you are to stay in the room we'll need you to be completely calm. You may hold her hand."

Max said nothing. He didn't think he was capable of saying anything but he stepped forward between two nurses and took Christine's hand in his. Dr. Mulholland worked fast, she ripped into Christine's uterus and pulled the baby out. The baby was then rushed to another station where a team of pediatric surgeons worked on it – Max didn't even know if it was male or female – while another team of doctors worked to stem Christine's bleeding and prevent her from bleeding out on the table. Max stepped back and let them work, praying to whomever was listening to just save his family.

There was a tense moment when the machines around Christine began beeping in a very alarming manner and Max wanted to scream at the doctors to do something; make it stop. But he didn't want to distract anyone from their work. He looked toward the baby's table, where things looked calmer. They looked like they had done what they could for the child, so either it was okay or...

Max moved toward the child, his heart in his mouth. One of the doctors saw him coming and smiled.

"You have a baby girl," he said and moved out of the way so that Max could see. A tiny child lay on the bed, with a head full of curly hair and dusky skin. She looked upset, was moving her head about as well as her limbs as if looking for something. Her mouth was pursed as if she was about to cry.

"Can I hold her?" he asked the doctor.

"Not yet," he said indicating the various tubes and wires linked to the baby. Such a tiny thing to have so many things poking and prodding at her. Max leaned forward to stare at her; he willed her to open her eyes but they stayed willfully shut.

"Hey baby. It's okay. Daddy's here," he murmured softly. The baby stopped moving for a moment and Max's heart literally stopped beating. Then she continued with her movements and Max's heart swelled with a feeling he had never experienced before. It came from nowhere and suddenly he was its prisoner. A powerful need to protect this little person came over him and he hunched over the crib, surrounding her with his presence.

"You're going to be just fine. And so is mama," he told her and smiled. The little girl opened her eyes and seemed to look at him for a moment. She had honey brown eyes, just like her mother's. It almost broke Max's heart to see it.

He straightened up, moving toward the other table. The frantic activity had calmed down somewhat, whatever the crisis was, it seemed to have passed.

"Is she alright?" Max asked Dr. Mulholland softly.

"I think she will be," she said smiling at him. Max nodded his head in gratitude.

"Thank you," he said feeling a huge lump in his throat and moisture blurring his eyes.

"Don't thank me just yet. She's not out of the woods. We'll watch her closer in the ICU for the next 24 hours to be absolutely sure. Your little girl will go to NICU. It's going to be a long day and night."

Max nodded his understanding. "Okay then. What can I do?" he asked.

"Pray I guess; if you're the praying type."

"Just tell me they'll be okay."

Dr. Mulholland looked at him, shaking her head. "Not in my hands but I can promise you we'll do everything in our power to give you back your family in one piece," she said.

"That's all I can ask," Max said and moved out of the way for them to move Christine and the baby out. He followed them until he was stopped at the ICU door. He turned around and walked back to the waiting room. He had calls to make.

He looked up and saw Martha standing by the waiting room table watching him come.
"How are they?" she asked looking anxiously at him.

Max tried to smile, he really did, but he couldn't quite manage it. Before he knew it, he was folded up on Martha's shoulder, weeping quietly.

"They're alive? Tell me that they are alive," she said holding tight to him.

'They're alive. Christine was bleeding pretty bad though. And the baby...they stuck all these tubes in her..."

"Her?" Martha said perking up. Max straightened up from her shoulder to look her in the eye.

"Yes. We have a baby girl."

Martha smiled. "I'm so happy for you," she said face beaming.

Max smiled back. "It's wonderful right?" he said wetly.

"It really is," Martha said. "And the babies will be just fine. Both of them. I promise you that."

"You promise?" Max repeated.

"Yes," Martha said. She pulled out her phone. "Now, I need to call some people and let them know."

"I think you should wait. Christine and...the baby won't be out of danger for twenty four hours."

"All the more reason why we all need to pray together on this one. We're going to form a prayer circle and keep them safe inside," Martha said.

Now Max wasn't what one would call a believer but hearing Martha say that made him feel much better about everything. Somehow he knew they would get through this in one piece.

*****

Christine and the baby came home four days later in good health. Christine was a bit weak with blood loss and the whole pushing a baby out of her body thing so Martha was staying over to look after her. The announcement of the baby's birth had been placed in the paper to notify anyone who needed to know. They didn't have a name yet so for now they were just calling her 'baby'.

"I think all this post baby expelling of fluids is like…thee most disgusting part of being pregnant," Christine told Max as they lay back in bed watching the baby sleep.

Max smiled. "It's funny you should say that because I don't think you've ever looked more lovely."

Christine gave him the most intense side eye. "Really? It's one thing to be supportive Max, it's quite another to tell blatant lies."

Max laughed out loud; Christine felt like she hadn't seen him laugh so much as he'd been doing in the last few days in all of the time she'd known him.

"I'm not lying. You're glowing...there's just something about you," he shrugged staring at her.

"You mean tiredness from waking up six times a night, leaking breasts and uncombed hair?"

Max's threw back his head and laughed. "Yeah, all that. And the hemorrhoids and everything else that you've been complaining about. It's all beautiful."

"You are so high on baby poop it's not even funny," Christine said watching him with an indulgent smile. She could see him wanting to burst into laughter again. Martha came into the room and she was carrying a tray with a bowl of porridge on it, a plate of waffles, and a flask of cocoa. On the tray was also an envelope.

"You have mail," she said.

"Who writes snail mail anymore?" she asked taking the envelope.

"Your mother apparently," Martha said putting the tray down on the foldout chair.

Christine moved her hand away from the envelope. "What does she want now? She already burned through that fifty k I gave her?" she asked slightly petulantly.

"Why don't you read the letter and avoid speculation?"

Christine sighed. "I don't know if I have the strength for her bullshit yet."

"Cordelia said she went off to better herself. Maybe this is a progress report," Martha said.

Christine snorted her disbelief but Max picked up the envelope from the tray and read the return address. "Jackson Mississippi? Why there?" he asked passing the envelope to her.

She shrugged, but her curiosity was piqued and she opened it. A single sheet of paper fell out and they both stared at it.

"Well? Aren't' you going to read it?" Max asked.

Christine sighed and picked up the paper and straightening it out to read it.

Dear Chris,

I hope this letter finds you well and healthy. I just heard from Uncle Andrew that you gave birth to a baby daughter and it filled me with such joy and pain I was compelled to write you. I don't know if you will read this, I won't blame you if you don't. I know I haven't earned the right to expect anything from you. I left you with my mother when you were very young. I suppose in your eyes, it was abandonment. In my eyes, at the time, I was doing what was best for you. My mother is much better at this mothering thing than I am. I think we both can agree on that.

But I digress. This letter wasn't meant as some sort of self-justification for my decisions. It was prompted by a sort of nostalgia for you and for the child you've just borne. I remember holding you in my arms. You were the most precious thing I had ever beheld, and you stared back at me like you knew who I was. I just wanted to protect you. I wanted the best for you.

Now you have a child of your own. Maybe you can understand a little bit that instinct to protect. That instinct to put your child's needs before your own.

Christine snorted with derision. "Wow. Talk about revisionist history," she said.

"Keep reading," Max said leaning back on the headboard, his hand on the baby's head.

Christine sighed but went on reading.

That instinct to put your child's needs before your own. To sacrifice for them and protect them.

Christine grimaced at Max who gestured for her to continue.

So I may be late, but I hope I'm not too late. I don't know if you know but I dropped Kevin. He's gone from my life as are all the toxic men I used to choose. I'm making better choices because I want to be better for you. I'm attending a cooking school here in Jackson. It's run by an old friend of mine, and I'm doing well. He has a job for me at his restaurant here if I pass all of my certifications. Your mama gonna have a legit job; that's something right? It's a start at least. I want to start loving myself more, so I can love you better. You and my grandbaby. Kiss the little girl for me. Tell her I'll see her soon.

All of my love.

Mom.

"What the fuck am I supposed to do with this?" she asked Max.

He shrugged. "Hey, at least your mother is willing to make an effort. My mother just complains and intrigues and tries to play games."

"There's no guarantee these are not games."

"There are no guarantees in life Chrissy dearest," Max said.

"Have I told you I really hate those nicknames you give me?"

"Several times," Max said picking the baby up quickly as she started to move around in preparation for fussing and crying. "We have to come up with a name for this little one before we give her a complex."

"Gwendolyne," Christine said.

"A real name," Max replied with a side smile.

"How about Gina?" she suggested.

"Gina...hmmm. I like it."

"You do?"

"Yes. Don't tell me it was one of your joke names."

"No, I actually like that name."

"Great. Gina it is."

"Gina Richards-Lestrange," Christine said trying it out on her tongue. "It's a good name."

"Yes."

"Ethew," Gina said and they both stared at her in shock.

"I think that was agreement," Max said.

"I think it was too," Christine agreed. "Now if only all our decision making was that easy."

"Decision making about? Your mother? My mother? We ignore them until they grow up."

"High five," Christine said. They high fived to their decision and then Max leaned forward with a laugh and kissed her.

"Speaking of decision making..." he said against her mouth.

"You are a randy French bastard you know that?"

"Hey...I'm not a bastard; my parents were married when I was conceived," he retorted.

"Oh really, well mine definitely weren't so I guess *I'm* the bastard," Christine said.

"Can females really be bastards? I'm never sure," Max said thoughtfully.

"The number of things you're never sure of could fill a small country," Christine scoffed.

"Don't be mean," Max sulked.

"Aww, my widdle baby," Christine said pinching his cheeks. "Did I hurt your feelings?"

"I don't know about my feelings but you're definitely giving me blue balls with your gratuitous display of boobage," Max said looking down at the offending organ.

Christine smiled. It was true that she'd exposed her breast as soon as Gina awoke because she knew it was a matter of time before she would be pining for some nourishment.

"You're going to have to get used to that."

Chapter 15

It was a total accident that they met. Max was in New York for a Formula One business meeting. The meeting had wrapped up early and he'd returned to his hotel to pack. He'd been invited to go out for the evening with the other executives but he was in a hurry to get home and see his wife and child. Gina was about to celebrate her two month milestone and Christine had just started to feel like her old self again. The inflammation on her left breast had subsided at last and Gina was only waking up three times a night now. They were finally finding a rhythm again and he figured it was time for them to get back to a sexual rhythm. He'd picked up a beautiful diamond necklace in the hotel gift shop that he was intending to give her as a two month milestone present as he persuaded her to spend some quality one on one time with him. Not that he thought he'd have to do a lot of persuading...he saw the way she looked at him when she thought he wasn't looking.

He was walking out with his bag packed heading to check out when he saw him. He had seen Rudy maybe twice in his life but he wasn't likely to forget. He stopped short, staring and then before he knew he meant to, his feet were taking him toward the man. He was sitting in the hotel bar, looking like he was waiting for someone.

"Rudy Sinclair as I live and breathe," he said coming up to the man and invading his personal space.

Rudy turned around to look at him in puzzlement. "Do I know you?" he asked the taller man.

"Probably not," Max said inkling his head to the side, "but you might remember my wife, Christine."

Rudy tensed visibly and Max smiled. "Ah, I see the name rings a bell," he said.

Rudy put up his hand, "Look, I don't want any trouble."

"Oh you don't? For someone who 'doesn't want any trouble' you sure do go looking for it."

"Hey listen, I didn't even *want* to speak to your wife that day. Your mother put me up to it."

Max stared at him, "I beg your pardon."

"That day...at the Ritz...I wasn't gonna try anything, I swear. I was just minding my business when your mother got in touch with me and asked me to seduce Christine again. She offered me too much money to turn down. My family keeps me on a tight financial leash," Rudy explained in a tone that could be described as whiny. "I couldn't really turn that down."

Max was frozen in shock. He'd approached Rudy maybe to just intimidate him, maybe to give him a piece of his mind – he hadn't been sure. And now the guy was throwing all this information at him that he hadn't been expecting and hardly knew what to do with. His mother had paid Rudy to seduce Chris? That would explain the timing and the pictures. The Ritz wasn't known for entertaining paparazzi. If he hadn't had such a visceral reaction to those pictures he might have figured out that something about the set up smelled, a lot sooner.

"Look, weirdo. I won't tell you again. Stay away from my family. If I see or hear of you anywhere near my wife again, there will be consequences and I guarantee you won't like them."

Rudy looked around. This was a five star hotel and security was tight; it wasn't like they would tolerate bar brawls. He smiled at Max. "And what will you do if I don't?" he challenged.

Max smiled. "Well let's see. I'll start with that cute little B&B you own in the Catskills; run it out of business. Then there is your adult entertainment distribution network. The backbone of your family's wealth isn't it? How would you like it if I dismantled that as well. Your chain of fast food restaurants? I'll run them into the ground. Do you think I can't do it? Try me."

Rudy stared at him. "All this over a piece of tail?" he sneered.

Max's eyes narrowed. "Now, I was going to let you go without administering a beat down because obviously you're a pathetic low life who isn't worth the oxygen it takes to keep you alive. But you know I can't let that pass right?" he said.

Rudy opened his mouth to say something obviously ill advised.

Max did not let him. Before he knew it, his hand had balled into a fist and he was connecting solidly with Rudy's right eye. The shorter man flew out of his seat and landed hard on his bottom, breathing hard and looking shocked. Hotel security began to close in and Max turned quickly, hands above his head and walked to reception as their eyes followed him.

"I'd like to check out now," he said to the receptionist. She looked extremely flustered but took his black card and ran it and then returned it to him. A porter was waiting with his bags and a driver had already been summoned to take him to the airport. Max added a generous tip for the 'damage to the bar' and then walked out of the hotel and left. Nobody tried to stop him.

*****

"Honey I'm home!" he called as he came in the door. They had moved to a five bed-roomed bungalow in its own compound when Christine was five months pregnant and they'd only just finished moving in properly. He walked through the living room looking for his wife but the house was silent. It was only as he crossed right over to the other side that he saw them through the floor to ceiling windows, sitting outside on the grass. Gina was lying on a blanket, kicking her legs and gargling to herself while Christine sat cross legged next to her, doing some light yoga and watching her daughter.

"Hey beautifuls," he called through the window.

Christine turned around and beamed at him.

"Hey you. Back so soon? I wasn't expecting you till tomorrow."

"Disappointed?" he asked leaning on the door jamb.

"Not even a bit," she said with a grin. He stepped through the door and walked to them, dropping to the ground on the other side of his daughter.

"Hello darling," he said leaning down to kiss Gina on the forehead. She gargled happily, looking up at him like she was really pleased to see him. Max ran his fingers through her curly brown hair and smiled. Then he looked up at Christine.

"Hello darling," he said and leaned over his daughter to kiss his wife.

"Hi. I like that nickname," she murmured.

"Oh. I'm so relieved," Max said with a wry smile.

Christine picked up his left hand. "What happened?" she asked. The bruises were still visible where his knuckles had connected with Rudy's eye.

"Got in a fight," Max said shortly.

"Uh huh?" Christine said encouragingly.

"You should see the other guy," Max evaded.

"Black eye?" she asked.

"Yep," Max said with satisfaction.

"Did he deserve it?" Christine asked.

"Absolutely, one hundred percent."

"Wow, that sure huh?"

"Yep," Max said.

"Okay then enough with the one syllable conversations. How was the meeting?"

"The meeting went well. We discussed new designs for the cars where we can collaborate. It was productive. We'll need to set up a division in A&R to deal specifically with this batch of cars for next season. It should be interesting."

"It sounds fun," Christine said ruefully.

Max smiled at her. "You know if you want to join our A&R team all you have to do is say."

"Don't tempt me," Christine said.

"Come on, we have far better benefits than that crappy job you have with the city," he coaxed.

"Hey. It's not a crappy job."

"Fine. But you can do better is all I'm saying."

"Fine. I'll think about it."

*****

Christine got back from putting Gina down to find Max in the kitchen, cute apron in place, serving dinner onto plates. Judging by the look of things or rather the smell of them, it was quite a feast. There was no way Max had time to cook it in the time it took her to bathe and put Gina down to sleep.

"Take out?" she asked.

He grimaced, "I was hoping you wouldn't notice that part."

"Okay, I'll pretend I haven't. Wow, lovely dinner you've made there Max. I didn't know you were such a culinary expert."

"Craddock taught me," Max said.

"Craddock did huh? That's so great. I'll be sure to compliment him when he comes back from leave."

"You do that. Sit sit," he said as he pulled out a chair. She sat in it, wondering if she should get up and maybe go change her shirt at least. This was clearly supposed to be a date.

Max removed his apron and put it aside and then sat across from her.

"So, I thought we would toast to two months of parenthood as well as six months of me being without any symptoms," he said producing a bottle of non-alcoholic sparkling cider.

"Yay for us," Christine said digging into the parmesan chicken and rice. Max poured them both a glass and they toasted to two months of parenthood. They drank and then toasted again to Max's continued wellness. Next, they toasted the disappearance of inflammation on Christine's left breast and then the fact that breastfeeding was so awesome as a slimming agent. Their toasts continued to get more extravagant and ridiculous even though the cider was non-alcoholic, they still felt quite drunk on each other.

After the chicken and rice, Max produced a chocolate fudge cake so rich it had Christine moaning in orgasmic delight.

"You are the most awesome husband ever," she said.

"Are you glad you married me or what?" he asked.

"Best marriage of convenience ever," Christine said raising her glass and grinning. Max though, abruptly stopped smiling.

"What?" Christine asked.

"I'd like to think that we mean a bit more to each other than that," he said.

Christine stared in surprise. "We do. Of course we do. We're great friends for one thing."

"Only great friends?" Max asked.

"And awesome lovers," Christine pointed out. Max still wasn't smiling. In fact, he was looking ever more miserable.

"Do you still love Rudy?" he asked seemingly out of the blue.

"Of course I don't. Why would I?" she asked in surprise.

Max gave her a look.

"Hey, you can't hold past transgressions against me. I was a young innocent girl who didn't know any better. Now I'm an old lady with a kid. I have common sense now."

"That's great. So...you're not in love with...anyone," Max said still with that strange look on his face.

"Well...I don't know. I might be in love with you," she said.

Max stared at her, "You might be?"

"I might be. There is a strong possibility."

"What makes you think that?" Max asked moving closer to her.

Christine shrugged. "Well, it might be your thoughtfulness. You're always so solicitous of mine and Gina's welfare. You look at me like I'm the most gorgeous thing you've ever seen even when I know I'm gross. You don't complain about waking up in the middle of the night to clean poop off your daughter. You love my grandma even more than me...I could go on forever," she said.

"Well, when you put it like that," Max said with a shrug and a grin.

Christine looked at him. "And what about you? Are you in love with anyone?"

Max shrugged. "I might be too old for that kind of shit."

"Oh really? Too old?" Christine asked.

"Yeah I mean, that sunshine and rainbows stuff...isn't it for eighteen year old virgins with pink rooms and teddy bears?"

Christine laughed. "Are you trying to call me an eighteen year old virgin with a pink room and teddy bears?"

"Obviously not."

"But you want me to be in love with you..."

"I prefer to know I'm the only guy you're thinking of. Is that a crime?"

Christine shrugged, "I guess not."

Max put his hand on her thigh, "Speaking of things I want..."

Christine smiled. "Yes?" she prompted.

"Come to bed with me?"

*****

He carried her to the bedroom and laid her down on the bed, looking down at her with that look in his eyes that she loved.

"You're beautiful," he said.

"Says you," she replied.

He climbed on top of her, straddling her middle as he unbuttoned her shirt. She lay back arms spread wide and let him have his way with her. As he opened her shirt, he ran his fingers all over her skin, touching, squeezing, savoring the feel of naked flesh under his hands again.

"I've missed this," he said.

Christine smiled. "Me too," she said. He leaned down to kiss her and she opened for him, taking him into her mouth and pulling him down on top of her without so much as touching him with her hands. He leaned into her, pressing his whole body down on top of hers, almost suffocating her. But she didn't protest the treatment.

She wanted it. She wanted him to claim her for himself in every way it was possible to. Disengaging from his lips she looked up at him.

"I want you in my mouth," she whispered. He stared at her in surprise.

"What?" he asked, to be sure he'd heard right.

"I. want. You. In. my. Mouth," she said slowly like he was retarded.

Max didn't have to be told twice, he was off her in a trice and divesting himself of his pants. Then he was back on her, straddling her chest this time as he placed his penis against her mouth. She opened wide and let him in and he pushed in as deep as he could go with a long drawn out moan that spelled out her name.

"Chriiistttiiine," he groaned.

She made no response as her mouth was full of him. She sucked at him, first gently and then more roughly. Running her tongue up and down and then around his shaft, tasting every part of him.

"Aaaahhh," he moaned as he arched into her mouth. He touched her mouth to make her open wider just like she did when she was breastfeeding Gina and it made her laugh. She did open her mouth though and he pulled out.

"I wanna come inside of you," he whispered sliding down her body and licking down her chest. His hands caressed the sides of her legs, up and down, gently, creating currents of electricity all over her body. She lifted her head to kiss him, savoring the taste of him in her mouth and the hunger she could feel in his body. As she ran her hands over his back she could feel the tenseness of his muscles, straining toward her; his legs were shaking as they intertwined with hers and his pelvis thrust forward of its own volition rubbing against her with urgency.

"I think you're the one not interested in foreplay this time," she murmured into his ear.

He laughed into her skin. "You're not wrong there. It has been too long."

"Thank you for waiting until I was ready," she said.

"You are so welcome," Max replied covering her mouth with his and sucking her tongue into his mouth. They kissed for a long time enjoying the sensation of touch and taste even as they banked the urgency stemming from the possibility of Gina waking up at any moment.

"Fuck me Max," she whispered. Max's whole body shuddered.

"God I love it when you talk dirty to me," he said into her neck.

"I want you to penetrate me, take me deep and hard, mark me. I want you to do me so hard I'm walking funny for a week," she whispered into his ear. He moaned loudly, spreading her legs roughly and pushing into her rough and hard.

"Fuck me till I can't walk Max," she continued and he let out a pained sound, pounding her hard into the mattress. He was beyond reason; his body just took over and he let it have its way, pumping into her with no coordination or care; just letting his body take them where it may.

"Max," she groaned hoarsely. "Max my love, fuck me good."

Her words seemed to goad him to greater effort, he clutched the pillow on either side of her and went to town on her. Working his hips like pistons so he could go deep, driving her to extremes of feeling as she felt him so far inside she worried he might never find his way out again. Suddenly he flipped them over so she was straddling him and it was she who was riding him. He lifted and dropped her onto him, arching up to meet each thrust with a shove of his own.

"Chris," he groaned mouth spread in a rictus of effort. "Chris," he said again and his whole back arched off the bed as she felt him come inside her. Her body reacted to the inflow of fluid by clenching tight around him and she shuddered to her own completion soon after. They collapsed on the bed in a heap of languid satisfaction, smiling with happiness.

For a moment they lay there, unmoving, unable to so much as spare the energy to breath.

"Damn," Max said.

"Yeah I get it," Christine replied turning her head to grin at him. He looked back at her meeting her gleeful eyes with his. Suddenly the laughter died out of his eyes and he stared at her seriously.

"I love you," he said.

She stared at him, not sure she had heard right.

"Did you hear me?" he asked.

"You don't have to say that," she said.

"I know I don't have to. I want to. I mean it."

"You do?" she asked.

"Yes. I do," he said face so serious there was no way she could mistake him.

Christine turned to stare up at the ceiling.

"I...don't know what to say," she said.

"I understand if you don't feel the same way," Max said. Christine turned to look at him again.

"That's not it," she said.

"It's not?"

"No."

"Then what is it?"

Christine smiled. "All my life, I've wondered about myself you know? My mother abandoned me, Rudy abandoned me…I wondered what it was about me that was so unlovable."

Max opened his mouth to protest but she held up a hand to stop him talking.

"I've felt unlovable for a long time; I figured that having a child would be the key to getting someone to love me unconditionally. I guess that's why I agreed without too much fuss when you asked. I was ready for somebody to love me. I thought you and I would muddle along together amicably, be civilized and polite, take tea with each other and discuss our days, raise our child and call it a win," she said looking at him with a wry smile.

"The reality though…the reality has been something else again. Something totally different. It's been…utopia. I know that's an extreme word to use but that's how it has felt. Like…perfect. I can't really ask for more. I was contented…"

"And now?" Max asked, wondering where the hell this was going.

"Now you tell me you love me…and my bubble is burst," she said.

"Why?"

Christine shrugged. "It's too much. I feel like we're really testing fate here. We're doing so well, why taint it with unnecessary emotion?"

Max propped himself up on one arm. "Christine Alexandre Richards-Lestrange, did you or did you not say to me just this evening that you thought you might be in love with me?"

"I did," she replied.

"Were you lying?"

"Nope."

"So how can you say that this emotion is unnecessary?"

"Because it's one thing for me to love *you*. But you loving me back is..."

"Is what Chris?" Max demanded.

Christine shook her head and said quietly, "Too much to hope for."

"Well, could you possibly start hoping for it because I'm kind of already in love with you here and it's too late to go back."

Christine smiled, "Well, I did say I was all grown up now. I can deal with this."

"Yes you can," Max agreed.

"I love you Max," she said.

"Good. Because I love you," Max replied leaning forward and kissed her silly.

Of course Gina chose that moment to rejoin the party by screaming her head off.

The end.

But there's more:

If you enjoyed this ebook and want me to keep writing more, please leave a review of it on the store where you bought it. By doing so you'll allow me more time to write these books for you as they'll get more exposure. So thank you. :)

Get Free Romance eBooks!

Hi there. As a special thank you for buying this book, for a limited time I want to send you some great ebooks completely **free of charge** directly to your email! You can get it by going to this page:

www.saucyromancebooks.com/physical

You can see a the cover of these books on the next page:

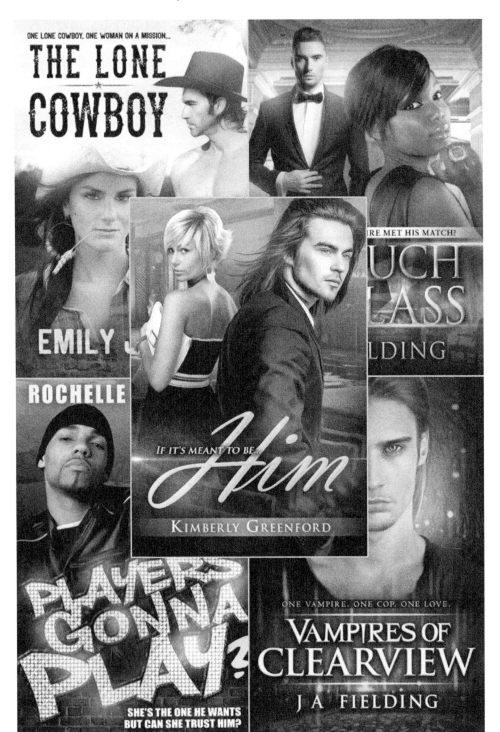

These ebooks are so exclusive you can't even buy them. When you download them I'll also send you updates when new books like this are available.

Again, that link is:

www.saucyromancebooks.com/physical

Now, if you enjoyed the book you just read, please leave a positive review of it where you bought it (e.g. Amazon). It'll help get it out there a lot more and mean I can continue writing these books for you. So thank you. :)

More Books By Cher Etan

To see more books by Cher Etan, simply search 'Cher Etan' under the books or Kindle book section on Amazon. :)

You can also see other related books by myself and other top romance authors at:

www.saucyromancebooks.com/romancebooks

Make Me Yours Preview

Here's a preview of my other book Make Me Yours (Search 'Make Me Yours Cher Etan' on Amazon to get it).

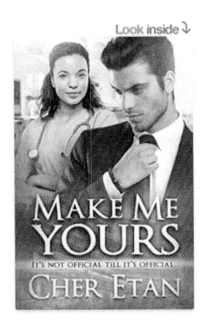

Description:

"Dean, make me yours..."

That's all Meaghan wants.

The two have always shared a mutual attraction, despite their upbringings being worlds apart.

Dean is an entitled billionaire with commitment issues.

Meaghan grew up in a deprived neighborhood and now holds a respectable position in a busy hospital.

Things between them are complicated; not properly together, but not seeing anyone else.

But things are about to get even more complex.

A new friendship formed between Meaghan and a hunky doctor has Dean brewing with jealousy.

Forcing the two to reassess their situation, can they do what's needed to make what they have work?

Or will Dean's commitment issues force the woman he's always loved into another man's arms?

The Story:

The country club was quiet at six am; only a number of golfers milling around waiting for their caddies. It was Dean's favorite time of day as he milled around waiting for Smith and his father to arrive. They used to be a foursome…before his own father's stroke had rendered him immobile. But they still kept up the tradition – Smith and Jonathan Winchester's way of saying that they were there for him he supposed – and Dean wasn't about to be the one to break it. He needed this; needed the connection to people with whom he could reminisce about a side of his father very few people saw. A hand clapped him on the shoulder and he turned around to see Smith smiling at him.

"Hey," he said.

"Hey man, ready to go?" Smith asked. His father was strolling toward them in conversation with his caddy. He'd had the same one for nigh on twenty years now. He no longer worked at the club but turned up for the game. He was part of the tradition too. Dean sighed, his heart heavy yet soothed by the presence of his friend; his family really, if one wasn't such a stickler for blood. Smith frowned at him.

"What's wrong?" he asked.

Dean looked up at him smiling at how well his friend knew him, "Nothing. The usual." He said and Smith nodded like Dean had made perfect sense.

"How's Poppy?" he asked next, eyes already ready to commiserate.

Dean shrugged, "It's been quiet. Too quiet. She hasn't hounded me once this week about ruining the family name or destroying our lives or giving her a stroke too...its making me tense."

"You think she's up to something?" Smith asked smile widening into a grin.

"Isn't she always?" he replied.

"Could you ask Bella if she's maybe heard anything on the bitch circuit about what my mother and Samantha could be planning?" Dean pleaded.

"What? You don't think the surprise birthday party they threw you was enough?" Smith asked laughing outright. "Oh my God your face – I'll never forget."

"You can laugh...I'm the one who had to deal with the fallout," Dean glared at him, "Although Meaghan was surprisingly cool about it. Didn't so much as freeze me out of her bed or anything."

"Oh, now that there *should* worry you," Smith retorted still snorting with laughter.

Dean shrugged, "Mmm, I don't know, Meaghan knows how I feel about her. And she knows that my mom and Samantha are trying to sabotage us. I don't think she'd willingly fall into one of their traps – she's not stupid."

Smith smiled. "And you guys still in love? The shine hasn't faded from the relationship? It's been six months after all. That's like...four years in dog years," he said tongue in cheek.

Dean looked seriously at him and sighed, "Man, I'm in trouble."

"Why?" Smith asked although he suspected he knew.

"Because this is the real thing," Dean said looking downcast and forlorn.

Smith nodded his head in agreement, "Yeah, it's kinda obvious you got it bad."

"I don't know what to do man," Dean confided.

"Don't know what to do about what?" Jonathan Winchester asked coming up alongside them.

Dean and Smith exchanged sidelong glances and then Smith said, "He's worried about Jeffrey Dad."

"Oh," Jonathan said with a clap on Dean's back. "Jeffrey is one of the toughest men I know Dean, he'll pull through this. You just wait and see."

*****

The object of Dean and Smith's conversation was just arriving for her shift at work. They'd call her in early because of a multi-car accident that had occurred on I-295, whose victims were being brought to the hospital. Meaghan was a bit nervous even though this wasn't her first rodeo; it *was* her first time dealing with an emergency of this magnitude. She knew she would have to think on her feet and react as fast as possible which was just the opposite of her style which consisted of thinking everything through carefully, weighing pros and cons and coming to a decision about how to proceed that way.

As she stepped in the hospital door, the first ambulance was screeching to a halt in front of accidents and emergencies and she hurried to her office to find her coat and wash her hands so she could get to work. The very first person brought in was a child with a broken leg and she was paged to deal with it. After that the day was just one long blur of blood and gore and death. Meaghan didn't think she'd ever worked so hard in her life but for every life that was saved there was one they could do nothing for and Meaghan felt every loss like a personal failure. When all the emergency patients were treated there were still regular patients waiting...it was a long day.

Her phone rang at the end of it and she looked down to see that it was Dean calling her. She stared at the name for a while wondering if she should answer but she was physically and mentally exhausted. There was no way she could summon enough energy to be the girlfriend right now. She barely had enough to declare herself a human being. So she clicked ignore then texted him to say she'd speak to him later, long day, blah blah. She put her phone in her pocket and sighed deeply then started when a cup of coffee appeared before her face held by the most delicate looking pair of hands she'd ever seen. She followed the hands to the face and her eyebrows went up in surprise. It was the new supervisor; Dr... Shelley or something. All the nurses were buzzing in excitement about him and calling him Dr. Sexy. He was a tall distinguished looking man with jet black hair going gray at the temples. His eyes were piercing blue and he tended to pin people down with them. She'd seen doctors lose their ability to speak when Dr Sexy, er, Shelley fixed his eyes on them. And now the same thing seemed to be happening to her.

"I thought you could use this," he said, his deep voice soothing her wounded spirit.

"Thanks," she squeaked not exactly sure why this guy was even speaking to her. They had been introduced at the meeting at which he was presented to them but had hardly exchanged two words since.

"I've been watching you Ms. Leonard," he drawled smiling at her.

Meaghan brows lifted at the 'Ms.'; she wondered if it would be incredibly rude or extremely flirty to say 'that's *Dr* Leonard to you'.

She didn't really know how these games were played.

"Why have you been watching me?" she asked instead.

"Because...you're going to make a great surgeon one day," he said fixing her with that stare and making her hand shake. Nerves; it was just nerves.

"Really?" she asked voice higher than usual. Dr. Shelley was a neurosurgeon of really good repute. The hospital was lucky to have him. He'd said he'd wanted to work here because he grew up in Queens. Meaghan had been really surprised to hear that – he certainly did not have the look of any of *her* neighbors...but it also gave her hope. If a fellow Queens resident could reach the heights that Dr. Shelley had then surely she had a chance too.

"Yes. Really. Plus I hear you grew up around here too," he said.

Meaghan stared at him suspiciously, she could be crazy but he really did sound like he was flirting with her. She couldn't remember what the nurses had said about his marital status though...either way; she had a boyfriend so it wouldn't fly. Should she just come right out and say so though or how the fuck did this work?

"I did grow up here. My mother worked as a nurse in this community and she inspired me to go into medicine," she said.

"That's cool. My dad was a mechanic and my mother is a house wife," he informed her.

"Oh," Meaghan said at a loss for how to reply.

"Well anyway, I wanted to compliment you on the exemplary work you did today. First rate. Was this your first crisis situation?" he asked.

"Yes," Meaghan said warmed by his words, "It was..."

Dr. Shelley nodded, "Yes, I know. The first one can be overwhelming. Would you like to sit down to some coffee and talk about it?"

"Yes I would," Meaghan said with relief. She definitely needed to talk to someone about her day and Dr. Shelley would understand her like neither Bain nor Dean would. He had been there; maybe he could give her some useful tips about how to get over the feeling of failure when one of her patients died; or how to cope with being immured in people's shit all day every day and then have to go home and smile at your loved one like everything was alright with the world. When you *knew* how fucked up it really was right this minute, where some kid was dying and you can't save them and you have to put on a brave face and tell their parents that there was nothing more you could do. It sucked ass.

*****

Dean drew up to the hospital anticipating surprising Meaghan by taking her home and cooking her dinner. He'd heard about the accident on I-295 and that patients had been taken to Mt. Sinai. So he'd called earlier to commiserate but she hadn't picked up and he knew it had been hard for her. He realized they rarely talked about the hard things; too many barriers to that, what with his family drama and their limited time together which he realized was mostly spent in bed. After his talk this morning with Smith he'd realized he didn't *really* know how Meaghan felt about the continuous attempts to sabotage them perpetrated by his mother and his ex-girlfriend. She always said she was fine with it; that she understood but maybe...

He pulled into the parking lot just in time to see her sliding into a blue SUV with a tall white older looking guy. The guy drove off and before Dean could think about it, he was following them. They didn't go very far; just to *La Trattoria*, Meaghan's favorite restaurant...the guy handed her out of the car – she was smiling at him – and they walked into the restaurant. Dean vacillated between wanting to drive off right away and wanting to find out who this guy was who *his girlfriend* seemed to have blown him off for. It seemed she wasn't too tired to talk to *him*. He snatched his phone off the console and sent Meaghan a text.

Where are you?

He tapped his foot, waiting anxiously for her reply. Willing her to tell him the truth. She didn't reply for a while and Dean was just contemplating stepping out of the car and going to confront her when his notifications pinged.

I'm at work. See you later?

Dean stared at the text, his eyes burning and his heart beat fibrillating dangerously.

She had lied to him.

*

Want to read the rest? Search 'Make Me Yours Cher Etan' on Amazon today.

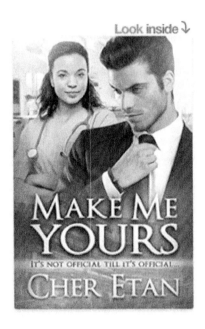

Printed in Great Britain
by Amazon